The pipe bomb exploded

Calvin James and Rafael Encizo had already ducked and covered their heads with their arms. McCarter had flattened himself against the stairs, but Katz had not anticipated the bomb.

A brilliant white light flashed from the explosion. Plaster and dust rained from the upstairs ceiling and flames danced through the blackened doorway where the dead terrorist lay. The corpse was charred, ribbons of smoke rising from burned flesh and clothing.

"Yakov!" McCarter cried when he saw Katzenelenbogen's body sprawled at the head of the stairs.

The Phoenix Force commander did not respond.

Mack Bolan's
PHOENIX FORCE

PHOENIX FORCE

Terror in the Dark

Gar Wilson

A GOLD EAGLE BOOK FROM
WORLDWIDE

TORONTO • NEW YORK • LONDON • PARIS
AMSTERDAM • STOCKHOLM • HAMBURG
ATHENS • MILAN • TOKYO • SYDNEY

First edition September 1987

ISBN 0-373-61331-8

Special thanks and acknowledgment to
William Fieldhouse for his contribution to this work.

Printed in Canada

1

The sun gradually descended behind a green hill beyond Dufferin Terrace. Tourists leaned along the handrail to photograph or just to watch a cruise ship that cut along the St. Lawrence River. A few evening workers sat on benches, eating sandwiches, barely glancing between the pillars at a view they took for granted.

Five men strolled the boardwalk, their stride casual, but their eyes shifting to and fro, constantly observing their surroundings. At first glance the five seemed to have nothing in common except their drab dark clothing and the canvas carrying cases slung over their shoulders. The eldest of the group was middle-aged, with a slight paunch and iron-gray hair clipped short and partially concealed by a wide-brimmed fedora. He walked with the assurance of a man of the world, a man who has seen much and done much and feels no apologies are necessary for how he has lived.

An acute observer might have noticed that the man wore pearl-gray gloves and that his right hand was stiff, the fingers unbending, as if he suffered from arthritis or partial paralysis. In fact, Yakov Katzenelenbogen had had his right arm amputated at the elbow in Israel during the Six Day War. He now wore a prosthesis.

Katz was a veteran of hundreds of battlefields. He had fought the Nazis in Europe as a youth, had participated in Israel's struggle for independence and later had fought to defend his chosen homeland. He had been a full colonel in the Mossad, Israel's principal intelligence network, and had worked on loan with the American CIA, the British SIS, the French Sûreté and the West German BND.

Yakov Katzenelenbogen was one of the most highly skilled and experienced warriors alive. He had fought in the ruthless realm of guerrilla resistance and in the shadowy, treacherous world of international espionage. He had taken part in the raw destruction of open combat and in the deadly cat-and-mouse game of stalking enemy terrorists in the Middle East and Western Europe.

Though no longer a young man, Katz had not retired. He was currently the unit commander of a unique commando team. The other four members of this special unit accompanied him now in Quebec City's colorful Old Town.

Walking beside Katzenelenbogen was Rafael Encizo, a muscular, handsome man with a trace of gray beginning to show in his jet-black hair. When his family had fallen victims to Fidel Castro's purge, the young Encizo had fled to the United States. Later, as a freedom fighter, he was captured by the Communists at the Bay of Pigs. Starved, beaten and tortured by his jailors, he never broke, and ultimately escaped.

Encizo returned to the United States and became a naturalized citizen with varied employment as a bodyguard, skin-diving instructor, treasure hunter and insurance investigator. None of these jobs had suited him as well as his present one with Phoenix Force.

Gary Manning, the tall man who followed his Israeli and Cuban teammates, was a native-born Canadian, familiar with Quebec. As an "observer" working with the Fifth Special Forces in Vietnam, he had developed his lethal skills as a demolitions expert and a master sniper. After Nam, Manning was recruited for an antiterrorist squad with the Royal Canadian Mounted Police, who sent him to West Germany to train with the elite GSG-9 unit. Later, he moved into the business world, and then into Phoenix Force.

Lagging behind the group was David McCarter, who had paused to light up a Player's cigarette, his cupped hand guarding the flame from the cold autumn wind. The tall, fox-faced Briton had spent his life mastering the skills he needed for the danger and adventure he thrived on. Born in the rough East End of London, McCarter was often sarcastic, sometimes short-tempered and occasionally downright rude; he would never fit into polite society, and had no desire to do so. As a youth the Cockney had joined the British army and later the elite Special Air Service. He saw action in Oman, Vietnam, Northern Ireland and Hong Kong, and was among the SAS commandos who took part in the successful raid on the Iranian embassy in London.

McCarter was a natural for Phoenix Force, where the success of every mission was vital to the interests of the Free World. It offered the talented SAS sergeant an opportunity to participate in greater adventures, greater dangers, for even higher stakes.

The only American-born member of the team was Calvin James. The lanky black former U.S. Navy SEAL team member had seen combat as a hospital corpsman in Vietnam, but his first survival courses had been in the streets on the South Side of Chicago as a youth. James received numerous decorations for valor before he left the service to study at UCLA on the GI bill.

Less than a year after James left the Navy, the tragic and senseless deaths of his mother and sister caused him to enlist in the San Francisco police, where he soon joined the Special Weapons and Tactics team.

When Keio Ohara, one of the original Phoenix Force members, was killed, James was abruptly drafted into the team, where he found the job that he had been born to do.

These were five men who at first glance seemed very different. But the differences were superficial; all were alike in spirit. They were men of action, devoted to protecting freedom and civilized values. Tyrants, terrorists, agents of totalitarian governments and international crime syndicates were among their targets. Their success rate was one hundred percent. Phoenix Force never refused a mission, regardless of the odds, and they never quit until the job was done.

That did not mean that none of them ever complained.

"I still say this mission is bloody politics," David McCarter growled as he fell in behind Calvin James.

"So you're still sayin' it," the black man retorted. "You sound like a goddamn parrot that only knows how to say one thing."

"But it's the bleedin' truth, and you know it," McCarter insisted.

"That doesn't mean we don't get tired of hearing you squawk about it," Manning told him, not bothering to glance over his shoulder at the Briton.

"It's politics, all the same," McCarter said with a pout, determined to get in the last word.

Nobody argued with the Briton. The mission he referred to certainly did not meet their usual standards. A small band of Marxist fanatics had slipped across the border from the United States to try to assassinate the prime minister of Canada. Nobody was sure of their motive. Hal Brognola suspected the fanatics would rather kill the President of the United States, but figured that the head of the Canadian government would be an easier target.

It was not that saving the life of the prime minister was not important enough for Phoenix Force, but sending the team to stop the assassins seemed absurd.

On the very day that the twelve American crackpots entered Canada, the FBI had learned about the scheme. The National Security Agency had located the extremists on the upper story of a small diner in Quebec that rented rooms to travelers, though at present it was closed. The diner was owned by Jean-Claude Mathis and his wife, Marie, both longtime supporters of the radical Front de Libération du Québec. The only occupants of the diner were the assassins and their host and hostess, so there was no danger to innocent bystanders.

And yet the NSA had not informed the Canadian authorities of the threat. CIA personnel at the U.S. embassy in Ottawa did not contact the RCMP or the Canadian SIS to offer information or assistance. Somebody close to the President—probably an advisor who believed cooperation with foreign governments, even friendly foreign governments, was less desirable than covert action—had convinced the man in the Oval Office that the American terrorists should be dealt with by the United States alone.

Hal Brognola, the head of Stony Man operations, had seemed almost embarrassed when describing the current assignment to the commandos. The best reason he could come up with to explain why the Canadian government wasn't informed and why Phoenix Force was being sent in was that the administration was worried that the U.S. national security apparatus would look inept. They wanted to put the would-be assassins out of action first, then tell the Canadian authorities that the danger had already been taken care of.

"We shouldn't even be here," McCarter continued to complain.

"Hey!" Manning rasped, annoyed. "I'm a Canadian, remember? I happen to think it's important to prevent those lunatics from assassinating my prime minister. I bet your attitude would be different if the royal family was in danger."

"Which member?" the Briton asked in a serious tone.

"Why the hell are a bunch of half-baked Marxists from the States planning to assassinate the Canadian prime minister, anyway?" Calvin James wondered aloud.

"Why did Hinckley think he'd impress that actress when he shot Reagan?" Rafael Encizo said with a shrug. "Some of these people are just plain nuts. Maybe what they do makes sense to them, but it sure as hell doesn't to anybody else."

"It's not our job to analyze them, thank God," Katz commented as they passed a series of novelty shops, antique stores and bakeries. "And we'd better change the subject. Someone might overhear us."

"*Oui,*" Manning replied, switching easily to French, the primary language of Quebec. "*Je me plais à cette ville.*"

"*Que c'est belle,*" Katz agreed. He spoke six languages fluently, including French.

"Crap," Encizo muttered. He was the only member of Phoenix Force who did not understand French. "I hate it when this happens."

"You're not missing much, mate," McCarter assured him. "Just a lot of drivel about how great it is to be in the bleedin' country. *Quelle université préférez-vous, Roger?*"

"UCLA," James answered gruffly. "And I ain't gonna answer to Roger for a cover name. I just don't like it."

The five continued to chat in both French and English as they walked through the old town. The ornate buildings and multicolored canopies overlooking sidewalk cafés were reminiscent of eighteenth century France. Mounted on a wall was a sign bearing the political slogan, *Maîtres chez nous*. Many French Canadians wanted Quebec to become an independent state separate from Canada, but support for the separatist movement had dwindled in the eighties.

"Heads up," Katz warned as they approached the diner that was sheltering the hit team. "We're getting close."

"About bloody time," McCarter said with a snort.

The diner was sandwiched between a pawnshop and a leather-goods store. Blinds and curtains were drawn across the windows on both stories, and a sign in the front door stated in both French and English that the diner was closed.

"All right," Katz said thoughtfully, "David and I will go to the front door. The rest of you find a way in from the rear. Remember there may be sentries watching from the windows.''

"Right," Manning agreed. "You know, this could get kind of noisy. I think our boss wants it to be handled quietly."

"Brognola knows these things can't be dealt with by a few polite whispers," Katz replied. "After we take care of the terrorists, it's up to the NSA, CIA, or whoever to explain to Canadian officials why the U.S. handled the situation this way."

"Bloody politics," McCarter complained again.

"I'm glad he's going with you, Yakov," Encizo muttered as he followed Manning and James up the street.

Katz and McCarter waited five minutes for their teammates to get around the corner to the back of the diner. Then the Israeli and British commandos crushed their cigarettes underfoot and walked to the diner. McCarter noticed a curtain move at a second-story window.

"Sure hope all those supersleuths in the spy outfits know what they're talking about," the Briton whispered as they approached the door, referring to the information that had been supplied to Phoenix Force about the diner and its occupants.

"We'll find out in a moment," Katz replied. He shifted the canvas case from his shoulder to slide his left hand inside for his firearm.

"I can hardly wait," McCarter said. He, too, reached in his bag as he slammed his boot into the door, just above the knob.

The lock burst apart and the door swung open. Inside the diner, several figures darted among the tables and chairs, grabbing for automatic weapons. Katz and McCarter stood clear of the doorway, their weapons pointed through the opening. McCarter carried an Ingram MAC-10 machine pistol, and Katz held an Uzi subgun with a folding metal stock.

The Israeli fired a burst of 9 mm rounds into the ceiling, the Uzi rasping through a foot-long Interarms sound suppressor attached to the stubby barrel. Plaster dust showered the gunmen inside the diner.

"Haut les mains!" Katz shouted, then remembered that most of the terrorists were Americans, who might not understand French. "Drop your weapons and put your hands up!"

The gunmen inside ignored the order and raised their weapons. McCarter opened fire, parabellum slugs hissing from the silencer of his MAC-10. He shifted the aim of the compact Ingram blaster to spray the terrorists from left to right.

Two bullets slammed into the chest of a long-haired American cretin and tore his heart into useless pulp. A CAR-15 automatic rifle fell from the terrorist's quivering fingers as he tumbled away from a table and collapsed to the floor. Another gunman caught a 9 mm slug under the nose. The bullet severed his upper lip and split the maxillary bone to burrow into his brain.

Katz fired another salvo at the enemy. Most of the terrorists managed to duck behind cover in time to avoid the deadly swarm of parabellum rounds, but one guy did not get his head down far enough. His forehead jutted above the edge of a table, and a 9 mm slug punched into his skull at the hairline and spattered his brains across the floor.

McCarter plunged through the doorway and shoulder-rolled to a table and chairs for cover. A heavy-set man with slicked-down black hair parted in the middle rose behind the serving counter to fire a Canadian-made C-1 9 mm submachine gun at McCarter's position. Bullets splintered wood from the furniture protecting the Briton.

"You're a lousy shot, bloke!" McCarter shouted, but he did not raise his head to give the gunman a better target.

"Cochon!" the man behind the counter snarled as he triggered another salvo of C-1 slugs at the Briton's cover.

As Katz crossed the threshold he fired his Uzi. Three 9 mm projectiles nailed the French Canadian in the upper chest, tearing a gory hole in the hollow of his throat and a larger, messier exit wound at the back of his neck. The gunman fell as crimson soaked his shirtfront.

"Jean-Claude!" a woman's voice cried. A scrawny female in a baggy flower-print dress that flapped on her bony frame like sails in the wind darted across the room to the slain French Canadian.

Marie Mathis knelt beside her dead husband while the three remaining terrorists in the dining room considered their options. They could continue to fight, surrender or flee. Two decided to fight while the third chose to run. He waited for his comrades to start shooting at Katz and McCarter before he scrambled toward the kitchen door.

But there was no sanctuary in the kitchen. Manning, James and Encizo had smashed through the back door and had burst inside. Three American terrorists had been lurking there when the gunfight erupted in the dining room. The trio were fumbling for their weapons when the three Phoenix fighters exploded through the back door.

Manning entered first, an Uzi subgun in his fists. A startled terrorist whirled and tried to brace the plastic stock of his black-market M-16 assault rifle against his hip. Before he could pull the trigger, Manning's Uzi coughed through an Interarms sound suppressor and three 9 mm slugs blasted the guy's face into scarlet mush.

Manning dived for cover at the end of a heavy oak table designed for food preparation. The other two terrorists had turned their weapons toward his hurtling form. One clod opened fire with an old U.S. Army M-3A-1 submachine gun, a .45 caliber blowback action weapon that is difficult for an inexperienced gunman to handle, due to the abrupt "climb" of the barrel of the greasegun. The terrorist fired only two .45 slugs in Manning's direction, both bullets chipping wood from a chopping block at the end of the table. Then the terrorist lost control of the M-3A, which continued to chatter out rapid-fire slugs as the barrel rose.

While the guy with the greasegun emptied the magazine into the ceiling, his partner fired a Smith & Wesson .38 revolver at Manning. A 125-grain hollowpoint round sizzled past the Canadian's position and blasted into an oven door.

The creep with the revolver did not get a chance to improve his marksmanship. Calvin James aimed a S&W M-76 submachine gun at the triggerman and sliced him with 9 mm slugs from solar plexus to jawbone. The impact tossed the gunman backward to crash into a garbage can full of spoiled food and stained cartons. The dead man tipped the can over, spilling trash across the tile floor.

Meanwhile, the moron with the M-3A realized he had wasted all his ammo and stared with astonishment at the empty weapon in his hands. A bottom-of-the-barrel amateur, he had learned the little he knew about guns from the nonsense he saw on television, where machine guns fire indefinitely without reloading and make one invincible. He had planned to mow down a hundred Canadian cops with the greasegun and then return to the U.S., where he had hoped to off a couple of hundred more.

The panicked amateur displayed more TV mentality by throwing his empty weapon at Calvin James. The black warrior easily dodged the flying chunk of metal. He could have shot the dumbass terrorist as the guy charged forward and swung a boot, trying to kick James's M-76 from his hands, but the Phoenix pro shifted his weapon out of the path of the clumsy attack and launched a tae kwondo kick of his own.

James's foot swung in a rapid roundhouse stroke and crashed into the side of his opponent's jaw, breaking bone and teeth. The halfwit terrorist fell to the floor. James kicked him again behind the ear to make certain he did not wake up for a while.

"These dudes are pathetic," James muttered.

"They just don't make terrorists like they used to," Encizo commented as he entered the kitchen.

The panicked gunman who had fled from the battle in the dining room ran straight into the three members of Phoenix Force who had taken out his comrades in the kitchen. The terrorist gasped and tried to point his Mini-14 automatic rifle at the trio.

James and Encizo whirled and fired their subguns, and Manning joined in with his Uzi an instant later. Ten 9 mm rounds tore into the terrorist and propelled him back through the doorway into the dining room. Encizo followed the bullet-wrecked body and peered into the battlefield of tables, chairs and fresh corpses. He saw Katz and McCarter exchanging shots with a pair of gunmen who had turned over two tables and reinforced their shelter with some chairs.

The terrorists leaned around the edge of the barrier to fire their weapons at the British and Israeli warriors. Neither man realized Encizo had the muzzle of his Heckler & Koch MP-5 machine pistol pointed at their exposed backs. Suddenly, Marie Mathis saw Encizo. She grabbed her husband's C-1 blaster and aimed the Canadian version of a Sterling subgun at the Cuban commando.

"Yankee canaille!" she screamed, her tear-streaked face contorted with bitter rage.

Encizo had no choice. He triggered his MP-5 and shot the woman's face off. A trio of parabellum slugs popped open the back of her skull. What remained of her hair was sodden with gore as she fell back and slumped across the corpse of her dead husband.

The two triggermen at the furniture heap swung their weapons toward Encizo. The Phoenix fighter immediately ducked behind the serving counter as twin streams of 5.56 mm rounds burst from his opponents' CAR-15 rifles. Slugs punched into the aluminum wall of the counter and bit plaster above the shelter. One bullet shattered a heat lamp that hung over the counter top.

"Motherfucker!" one of the gunman snarled when he realized they had failed to ice Encizo.

The foul-mouthed terrorist had uttered his last obscenity. Manning suddenly fired his Uzi from the kitchen doorway, and two parabellum slugs through the teeth cleaned out the terrorist's mouth forever. A third bullet pierced the bridge of his nose and rearranged whatever brains he had.

The other terrorist pushed his slain comrade aside and fired a hasty volley at Manning. The Canadian ducked behind the doorway. The enemy slugs splintered wood and punched through plaster, but failed to tag the elusive Phoenix pro.

The gunman also failed to realize he had raised his head and shoulders above the shelter of the stacked furniture. David McCarter promptly took advantage of this mistake. The Briton's Ingram snarled three rounds that caught the terrorist in the nape of the neck and the base of the skull. The guy's CAR-15 clattered on the floor and he fell lifeless, what was left of his face smacking the tile with a splat.

By then a heavy-set black male with sunglasses and a bushy Afro and a slender young woman with long dirty-blond hair and steely blue eyes had appeared at the top of the narrow stairway leading to the second story. The black guy aimed a Winchester pump shotgun at McCarter and Katz, while the female savage braced the barrel of a C-1 subgun against the handrail.

Rafael Encizo opened fire with his Heckler & Koch from his position at the counter, hosing the terrorist pair with half a dozen rounds. Splinters flew from the railing, and blood spurted from the paunchy belly of the black gunman. He screamed and tumbled down the stairs, but the female recoiled to the wall. Her right arm hung useless, shattered by a 9 mm slug, but she held on to the C-1 chopper and managed to fire a poorly aimed salvo that raked the wall above Encizo's position.

"Eat it, bitch!" Calvin James shouted from the doorway as he raised his M-76 subgun and squeezed the trigger.

Three parabellums ripped an ugly line across the woman's chest. The C-1 slipped from her fingers and she fell against the rail, tumbling over and crashing to the hard floor below without uttering a sound.

"Cover me!" Yakov Katzenelenbogen urged as he dashed to the foot of the stairs.

"Wait a bleedin' minute!" McCarter complained as he chased after the unit commander.

Katz charged up the stairs, followed by McCarter. James and Encizo raised their weapons to cover the doors that lined the narrow corridor at the top of the stairs. Manning checked the terrorists who had already been put out of action. He only needed to cuff one of them.

As Katz reached the head of the stairs, a door opened. The figure in the doorway was barely five feet tall, his head mounted on stooped shoulders with no trace of a neck. Light flashed on the thick lenses of his steel-rimmed glasses as he touched a butane lighter to the stubby fuse of a crude pipe bomb.

"Fuck!" Encizo snarled as he fired at the terrorist.

James's M-76 also erupted, and both subguns blasted the bomber with 9 mm destruction. The fanatic's glasses burst, and blood flowed from his eye sockets as his body slumped to the floor.

Then the pipe bomb exploded.

James and Encizo had already ducked and covered their heads with their arms. McCarter had flattened himself against the stairs. Manning was in the kitchen, binding the wrists of the only surviving terrorist. Katz, however, had not seen the bomb until it was too late.

A brilliant white light flashed from the explosion. Plaster dust rained from the upstairs ceiling, and flames danced in the blackened doorway where the dead terrorist lay. The corpse was charred, ribbons of smoke rising from burned flesh and clothing.

"Yakov!" McCarter cried when he saw Katzenelenbogen's body sprawled at the head of the stairs.

The Phoenix Force commander did not respond.

2

Hal Brognola chewed an unlit cigar butt as he paced the tile floor of the waiting room. The Fed hated the antiseptic stink of hospitals, like the fumes from a bottle of rubbing alcohol. Christ, he thought. People probably choke to death on that stench.

As soon as he learned that one of the men of Phoenix Force had been injured, the head of Stony Man operations had arranged for a top-notch team of doctors to be on hand at St. Michael's Medical Institute in Arlington, Virginia. Brognola had found some comfort in the fact that Katzenelenbogen was able to be flown from the hospital in Quebec to the States for treatment. This suggested his wounds were not critical. But Brognola had not felt relief when he saw Katz rolled through the doors of St. Michael's on a stretcher, his eyes covered by white bandages.

"I still can't get over it," Calvin James muttered as he sat in a scoop-backed plastic chair, elbows braced on his knees, forehead pressed against the heels of his palms. "Those guys were just shit." He looked up at Brognola.

The Fed did not want to face him. He did not want to look at the faces of any of the men of Phoenix Force, but he knew he had to. None of them was being spared any torment during the ordeal, and Brognola would not cop out, either.

"You should have seen those clowns, Hal," James continued, gesturing hopelessly with his hands. "They were stupid, they were slow, they were the worst fuckin' amateurs you ever saw in your life."

"I know what you mean," Gary Manning stated as he gazed into the black pool inside his coffee cup. "Katz has gone up against the best in the business. Master spies, professional soldiers, international terrorists, the most clever and dangerous criminal minds—none of them were a match for Katz."

"Yeah," James said grimly, "but those shitty, untrained assholes took him out."

"Yakov isn't dead," Rafael Encizo told them, his voice a bit sharper than he intended. "He hasn't been taken out yet. Remember what happened to me last year? A bullet creased my skull and I was laid up in a hospital bed for nearly six months, but I got back in action."

"Yeah," David McCarter agreed, largely because he wanted to agree. "Katz is tough. He'll be right as rain after he's had time to recover."

"He's not gonna die, that's all we know for sure," James remarked. "In our business, you don't have to be dead to be out of the game."

A small man, whose head was bald except for a fringe of white hair, approached the group. He wore a white coat, and a stethoscope hung around his neck. A clipboard was pressed under his arm.

"Hello, gentlemen," he greeted them in a weary voice. "I'm Dr. Nolan, head physician of the team you called in, Mr. Brown."

"How is he?" Brognola, alias Mr. Brown, inquired tensely.

"Well," Nolan began, consulting the clipboard, "generally speaking, the patient is in good physical condition. Bruises, minor cuts, no broken bones or damaged arteries."

"Yeah," James said, a trace of annoyance in his tone, "I already told them all that."

"You're a doctor?" Nolan asked dryly.

"I don't have a medical degree," James answered, "but I've stitched up a lot of guys on the battlefield, and I've performed surgery a few times. I know enough to know when a man's injured and needs more than iodine and adhesive tape."

"Were you with him?" the doctor asked.

James nodded.

"He was lucky," Nolan stated. "From what the initial medical report records, and based on my own examination, you may have saved your friend's eyesight."

"Just applied some distilled water and a bandage," James replied. "But you said he *may* regain his eyesight?"

"We're not certain just yet how extensive the damage is," Nolan answered. "I'm sure I don't have to tell any of you that the human eye is a very sensitive and delicate organ."

"His eyes were bleeding," Manning said, shaking his head at the disturbing memory.

"There are fragments of metal in the eyes," Nolan confirmed, "but that's not really as bad as it sounds. The bleeding was mostly due to shallow cuts to the eyelids and at the very corner of the eye near the tear ducts. We're going to remove the fragments. In fact, they're setting up to do that now. I'll have to get back to the others in a moment."

"Sounds like you're telling us the injury isn't as bad as we feared," Brognola said hopefully.

"The shrapnel wounds aren't serious," Nolan assured him. "The damage caused by flash burns could be a different matter. Now, the cornea received a bit of bruising. Doesn't seem too bad, and even if it's worse than we think it is, cornea transplants are fairly common these days."

"You're worried about damage to the retina or the optic nerve," James stated.

"Exactly," Nolan confirmed. "And that's difficult to determine just yet. The retina and optic nerve are at the back of the eye. Damage to either can be permanent. In some cases surgery can restore a man's sight, and in other cases...well, there just isn't much we can do."

"What are his chances?" McCarter asked.

"Based on what we know so far," the doctor replied, "I'd say fifty-fifty, and I won't lean in either direction. Your friend might recover his sight entirely, or he might regain partial vision, or he could be blind for the rest of his life."

"Thanks for being honest with us, Doctor," Brognola sighed, tossing what was left of his cigar into a trash can. "I won't ask you to do what you can for Katz, because I know you'll do that anyway."

"We all will," Nolan promised. "I'm afraid the only thing you fellows can do now is wait and hope for the best."

The doctor disappeared up the corridor. Brognola jammed his hands into his pockets and looked at the remaining four men of Phoenix Force.

"You guys gonna be hanging around Arlington for a while?" he asked, already certain of the reply.

"Until we know for sure about Yakov," Manning replied, speaking for all four men.

"I figured that," the Fed said with a nod. "I'll need to be able to get in touch with you if an emergency occurs. Damn it! I wish there was more we could do for Katz."

"You've done everything you could," Encizo assured him. "I just hope we don't get a mission until he's on his feet and back to his eagle-eyed self."

"There's a chance that won't happen," James said, in a small voice. "Don't get your hopes too high, fellas. It can go either way."

"I can't imagine Phoenix Force without Katz," McCarter admitted. "The bloke's the best strategist and covert operator I've ever known. Sometimes I think he's got radar, his instincts are so good."

"We've all looked to him as sort of a father figure," Manning added. "He always keeps his cool, always remains an ultraprofessional. Yet we've relied on his understanding, wisdom and insight as much as we've admired his ability...."

"I hate to mention this," Brognola said, sighing, "but even if Katz regains his sight, he won't be the commander of Phoenix Force much longer. Two more years at the most."

"What the hell do you mean?" McCarter demanded, his voice rasping above a whisper.

"Shit, David," Brognola hissed savagely. "I don't like this, either, but the fact is Yakov is getting up there. How long do you figure he can keep working in the field?"

"He's as good as any of us," Encizo insisted. "In some ways he's better. His reflexes and stamina are better than most eighteen-year-old athletes, for Chrissake."

"His reflexes weren't good enough this time," the Fed stated, wishing he did not have to say it.

"That's not fair, Hal," Manning told him. "What happened to Katz could have happened to any of us. We've all been wounded during our Phoenix missions."

"That's a fact," James said, holding up his left hand to remind Brognola that part of the little finger had been wrenched off in a terrorist torture chamber.

"Yeah," Encizo added, as he extended his right palm to display the circular scar of a red-hot coin that had been branded into his flesh by the same torturers. "I also got shot through the lower shin in Israel, and I got laid up with that head wound during our mission in France. You figure I've screwed up too badly to stay with the team?"

"We've had our doubts," McCarter answered with a shrug.

"Shut up, David," Encizo rasped. "Don't forget you caught a bullet in the arm when we were in Greece."

"I was going to mention it," McCarter assured him. "The fact is, Hal, we're just flesh and blood. None of us are perfect, but Katz probably comes closer to it than anyone I know."

"Look," Brognola insisted, "I admire and respect Katz as much as you guys do, but bear in mind that nothing lasts forever. Maybe we'd better just worry about one crisis at a time. If Katz gets through this ordeal okay, we'll consider the age factor later."

"Gee," Manning began dryly, "that makes us feel a hell of a lot better, Hal."

3

Martin Bowie had finally saved enough money to take his family on a real vacation, a trip outside the continental United States. Like many other Americans, however, Martin was worried about terrorism in Europe. A holiday in Central or South America was vetoed for a similar reason. The damn Sandinistas or whoever might start killing tourists at the drop of a sombrero.

The Bowie family was trying to decide between Hawaii and the Bahamas when Martin came upon a travel brochure for a safari vacation in Africa. Martin had always wanted to see Africa, and the kids were excited by the idea. Ellen, his wife, got interested after she saw *Out of Africa* with Redford and Streep. The stories of political unrest in South Africa worried the Bowie family, but they were relieved to learn the apartheid conflict did not involve the country of Kenya.

The Bowies really did not know much about Africa. Until they planned their safari, they had not realized Africa was the second largest continent and consisted of more than fifty countries and numerous offshore islands.

Kenya was located far from turbulent South Africa. Although Ethiopia was at Kenya's northern border, and the Bowies knew of the famine there, they decided a trip to Kenya would be an exciting adventure that would not expose the family to danger. Their itinerary would avoid any places where emaciated children might be seen. After all, one did not want to feel depressed during a vacation.

When they arrived at Jomo Kenyatta Airport in Nairobi the Bowies were surprised to find it was remarkably similar to airports in the United States. Nairobi was a modern city with skyscrapers, apartment complexes and office buildings. Smiling ebony faces greeted the family everywhere. Most of the citizens of Nairobi wore Western-style clothing, and many of them spoke English as well as the official language of Swahili.

The Bowie family were pleased they had come to Kenya. The Africans did not seem much different from Americans. Martin felt certain the trip would be a wonderful learning experience for Bobby and Jenny, who were discovering that people were the same no matter where they lived. Martin Bowie had always believed that the way to find peace in the world was for people to get to know each other. Through mutual understanding, he figured one day there could be a world community that would abolish nuclear weapons and war.

Of course, he knew the League of Nations and later the United Nations had been created to ensure world peace after the two world wars. Neither organization had been very successful at preventing international conflicts. Yet Bowie still believed all the people of the world could become friends and so influence the politicians to maintain the peace.

His theory had two major flaws. First, it was not only physically impossible for all the people of the world to meet one another, let alone become friends, but it would also require them to overcome all religious and racial prejudices, suspicion and fear and to somehow bridge the problem of language. Second, most of the world's governments did not truly represent or carry out the wishes of their citizens.

But although Martin and Ellen Bowie were impractical idealists, their hearts were in the right place. The family was generous and pleasant toward the Kenyans they encountered. When they experienced language problems they communicated patiently with gestures and charades, which led to much good-natured amusement and a remarkable degree of understanding by all concerned.

The safari the Bowies went on was a journey in a tour bus through Tsavo National Park. The bus traveled along the well-worn paths of the Kenyan savanna, where magnificent animals roam free.

The tourists were not disappointed by the sights along the way. A small herd of elephants grazed among the tall grass, the huge beasts barely disturbed by the familiar vehicle loaded with sightseers. A great bull with long curved tusks and enormous ears faced the bus. His slender tail twitched slightly as he spread the twin sails of his ears. Elephants have poor eyesight, and rely largely on their senses of hearing and smell.

The elephant did not appear to regard the bus as a threat, but the scent of people made him uneasy. The tourists meant the elephants no harm, and the rangers who patrolled the park brought the animals food during droughts and protected them in other ways that the beasts could not comprehend. Yet although all animals in the national park were protected by law, poachers still stalked the beasts illegally, usually not for food, but for their skins or their heads or—when elephants were the targets—for ivory.

The poachers sold their trophies to black-market dealers, who in turn supplied markets in Hong Kong, Thailand and elsewhere. A genuine leopard belt was worth several thousand dollars, the head of a lion with a full mane even more. A single elephant tusk sold for more than a thousand dollars, and an umbrella stand fashioned from an elephant's foot made an expensive curio that individuals of questionable taste would pay a few hundred dollars to possess.

The bull elephant finally decided the tour bus was harmless and joined his harem to gorge on the abundant vegetation. Two young calves played near the massive legs of their mothers, much to the delight of

the Bowie family, who eagerly photographed the frol-
icking animals.

The bus passed a herd of zebra and a few towering
giraffes that were dining on the leaves of a tall acacia
tree. A lone cheetah crept through the tall grass. The
long lean cat conserved energy and tried to stay up-
wind from his intended prey. Yet some of the zebras
sensed danger.

The cheetah suddenly bolted toward the herd, a
streak of blurred spots and tawny fur. The zebras took
flight in panic. The giraffes were startled by the
movement, but did not choose to run. The single cat
would not attack a full-grown giraffe, which could
defend itself with long legs and sharp hooves.

Indeed, the cheetah had already chosen its target, an
older zebra that was less agile than the younger animals. The cheetah stayed on the heels of its intended
victim and even ignored a couple of slower zebras that
it darted past in its single-minded chase.

Suddenly the cat leaped, seizing its quarry by the
neck. The tourists on the bus gasped, and a few cried
out in horror as the spotted predator brought down the
striped horselike creature. The kill was quick. There
was nothing personal about the cheetah's attack. It
was simply necessary for survival.

The rest of the zebra herd continued to flee. Even
the giraffes were unnerved by the scent of fresh blood,
and galloped from the scene. The cheetah tore at the
white-and-black hide and eagerly gulped down chunks
of meat. Its yellow eyes peered suspiciously at the tour

bus, as if the cat thought the vehicle might try to rob it of its kill.

"Oh, God!" Ellen moaned, burying her face in Martin's shoulder. Violence of any kind upset her.

"It's nature's cycle, dear," he said as he stroked her hair. "Survival of the fittest . . ."

"I didn't want the children to see something like that," she whispered harshly. She was so distressed she hadn't noticed that Bobby and Jenny were watching the cheetah with fascination instead of horror.

The bus continued to roll through the park, passing several other animals, including a small herd of graceful reddish-brown impalas. The long curved horns of the handsome males resembled lyre-shaped crowns. The tourists' cameras were busy.

The tour lasted until dusk. In the early evening, the bus drove from Tsavo National Park to Kibwezio, where it parked at a split-level ranch-style restaurant with wide windows and a breathtaking view of Mount Kilimanjaro in the distance. The tourists poured into the restaurant and found places at wooden tables.

"I hope our pictures turn out," Ellen remarked, slipping the strap of her camera from around her neck.

"Especially the pictures of that leopard ripping up the zebra," Bobby said with a smile.

Ellen opened her mouth and clamped a hand over it, her eyes wide with horrified accusation. Martin quickly took her other hand. He frowned at the children and shook his head.

"I don't think we photographed that," he told Bobby.

"Oh, I did!" Jenny said cheerfully, holding a little 110 mm pocket camera. "And it was a cheetah, not a leopard. I remember seeing them on a *National Geographic* show . . ."

"You've got a good memory, sweetie," Martin told her, "but I don't think we should talk about this at the table."

"Is Mom gonna puke?" Bobby asked, his voice revealing the bewilderment of a child who knows what he sees, and does not understand the unseen factors that upset some adults.

"I'm fine," Ellen assured the rest of the family. Just then, a waiter in a red jacket approached and placed menus on their table.

"Do they serve zebra?" Bobby asked.

Ellen paled.

Martin held a finger to his lips and hushed his son, then glanced up in surprise as a shadow blocked the light of the overhead lamps. A tall, heavily muscled black man stood by the table. His yellow teeth gleamed in his dark chocolate face as he smiled at the Bowies. The man wore a black turtleneck shirt, and Martin wondered if he was uncomfortable in the eighty-five-degree heat, which seemed twenty degrees hotter because of the humidity. Then he decided native Kenyans were accustomed to the climate.

"Excuse me," the black man said politely. "Mr. Bowie?"

"Uh...yes," Martin replied, surprised that the stranger knew his name. "What can I do for you?"

"Nothing at all, Mr. Bowie," the man assured him, still smiling. "You have a telephone call. Long distance from the United States."

"Here?" Martin asked with raised eyebrows, wondering who the African was. He was not dressed as a waiter. Perhaps he was the restaurant manager.

"Oh, yes." The African nodded as he gestured toward a corridor that extended beyond the dining room. "You'll find the telephone at the end of the hall and to the right."

"Who would call us here?" Ellen wondered aloud. "How did they know where to find us?"

"Perhaps your hotel forwarded the call," the stranger suggested. "If you're in Kenya as part of a tour, the hotel would know you'd be here about this time. Yes?"

"It's probably Davidson," Martin said as he rose from his chair. "I bet he's having trouble with the Lawrence account."

"Oh, Marty!" Ellen sighed. "Not on our vacation...."

"Don't worry," Martin assured her. "I'll be right back."

"If you'll follow me, sir," the stranger invited.

He led the way along the corridor and Martin Bowie followed. The American noticed a small walkie-talkie clipped to the man's belt. Maybe the guy was some kind of security officer.

"Uh, I'm curious," Martin said. "How did you know who I was?"

The man seemed a bit surprised by the question. "Oh, well, the caller described you quite well, Mr. Bowie. Described your entire family, in fact."

They passed two doors with symbols that identified them as rest rooms. The stranger pointed at another door at the end of the corridor.

"The phone is through that door, sir," he explained.

"Okay, thank you, Mr. . . . ."

"You're welcome, sir." The African smiled.

Martin opened the door, surprised to see that it led outdoors. It was dark now. He could see nothing but shadowy bushes and a strip of star-studded sky through some tree branches. He did not see a telephone.

Without warning, a strong hand shoved into the small of Martin's back and pushed him across the threshold. The American gasped with surprise as he stumbled forward toward the bushes.

From the shadows a dark shape appeared. Martin glimpsed only a head and shoulders and arms that swung toward him. He raised his own arms to protect himself. Sharp metal raked his flesh. Blood splashed his shirt, and he opened his mouth to scream.

Then something seized Martin's throat. It gripped like a hand, yet blades pierced skin and muscle. Martin saw the eyes of his assassin, wide brown orbs that glowed with excitement. The terrible claw hand at his throat pulled hard, tearing open his flesh and severing his windpipe with a single stroke.

Martin Bowie's last conscious thought was that he was about to die and he didn't know why anyone would kill him.

"EXCUSE ME, Mrs. Bowie?" said the polite black man in the turtleneck shirt as he returned to the tourists' table.

"Where's Marty?" Ellen asked with a frown.

"Still on the phone, ma'am," the African replied. "He asked me to fetch you. Whoever the caller is, apparently she wants to talk to you as well."

"She?" Ellen smiled. "It must be my mother. She was worried about us taking a trip to 'darkest Africa.' We told her Kenya was probably safer than New York or Los Angeles."

"I wouldn't know, ma'am," the stranger said. "If you'll follow me, I'll be happy to take you to your husband."

"Thank you," Ellen said as she rose from her chair. "Now, you kids behave until we get back."

"Sure, Mom," Bobby promised, sipping a glass of milk.

"Can I talk to Grandma?" Jenny asked.

"I don't think she'll be on the phone much longer, dear," Ellen replied. "Long distance to Kenya must be terribly expensive. I'll tell Grandma hello from you both."

Ellen followed the man in the turtleneck through the hallway to the door at the end of the corridor. The African opened the door for Mrs. Bowie. She gazed into the night.

"Your husband is waiting for you outside," he announced.

"Are you sure?" She frowned as she approached the threshold.

"I assure you, ma'am," the African said, smiling, "he isn't going anywhere."

He suddenly shoved her outside. Ellen yelled with surprise as he quickly shut the door. He placed his ear to the crack and heard Ellen Bowie cry "No!" Then there was a liquid gurgle and the tearing sound of ravaged flesh.

"Goodbye, Mrs. Bowie." The man chuckled as he opened the door and calmly stepped outside.

4

"It's sort of nice having all you guys in Arlington," Hal Brognola commented as he carefully selected a panatela. "You got here a lot faster."

Gary Manning, Calvin James, Rafael Encizo and David McCarter had been summoned to Stony Man headquarters, at a secret site in the Blue Ridge Mountains. The four Phoenix Force commandos had met with Brognola in the Stony Man war room many times in the past, but this was the first time they had assembled without Yakov Katzenelenbogen.

"I sure wish we were all in Arlington for a different reason," Encizo commented. "What's up, Hal?"

"What we all hoped *wouldn't* happen until we knew one way or the other about Yakov," Brognola answered. "Phoenix Force is needed for a mission. The President wants you guys to handle it because it seems similar to a job you handled a couple of years ago. I told him one of the team is out of action, but he still wants you for the mission."

"What's the problem?" Manning inquired as he poured himself a cup of coffee.

"There's been a rash of murders in Kenya," the Fed answered, checking a file folder as he spoke. "The victims have been Americans, British and a couple of West Germans. A few have been businessmen involved in trade or sales in Kenya, the rest have been tourists—most recently, Mr. and Mrs. Martin Bowie of Concord, New Hampshire. They were vacationing in Kenya with their kids. Somebody killed the adults right outside of a restaurant. They were found with their throats torn out. The children were spared."

"They're orphans, and their lives have been ravaged as surely as the bodies of their parents," Encizo stated, recalling the murder of his own parents by the Communists in Cuba. "The children weren't spared. They never are."

"Hal," James began thoughtfully, drumming his fingers on the table top, "you said their throats were torn out, right? Has that happened in every murder we're talking about?"

"Yeah," Brognola confirmed. "The murders were so brutal, the bodies mauled so terribly, that at first the authorities thought the tourists had been killed by wild animals. Maybe a man-eating lion or a crazed leopard. Some of the killings have occurred in the capital city of Nairobi, but they still thought the murderer must be a beast and not a man."

"Man can be the most savage beast of all when he puts his mind to it," McCarter remarked, lighting up a Player's.

"The murders in Kenya sure support that theory, David," Brognola stated. "The killers used steel claws, ripped up their victims like a big cat might."

"Did they show *Nightmare on Elm Street* in Kenya?" James asked dryly. "On second thought, I don't think they'd have to. The method of killing with artificial claws was practically invented in Africa."

"Bloody hell," McCarter groaned, staring up at the ceiling. "I knew this sounded familiar. I came up against a lunatic wearing a pair of leopard mittens with real claws when we carried out that raid on the Mardarajan embassy in London. The crazy bastard even had filed his teeth to be pointed like fangs."

"Right," James said, nodding. "A leopard man, a member of a leopard cult. Supposedly, leopard cults were fairly widespread throughout Africa at one time. Sounds like there are still a few of them around."

"We talked a little bit about this after the Mardarajan embassy raid," Manning recalled. "Do members of these cults worship leopards?"

"No more than a Christian worships a cross or a Buddhist worships a statue of Buddha," James explained. "Animism might not be considered among the major religions of the world, but millions of people still believe in it."

"Animism?" Encizo asked, not certain what the term meant.

"The belief that everything has a soul or a spirit," James explained. "Not just people, but animals, trees, rocks and rivers. Some even believe natural phenom-

ena—such as rain, earthquakes, night and day—have
their own spirits. So-called 'primitive' religions. Animistic groups aren't very organized, most don't have
any written scriptures—like the Bible or the Koran—
and few send out missionaries to try to convert others
to their beliefs. So, naturally, most people just dis-
miss them as a bunch of superstitious savages."

"I didn't know what animism was, either, until I
finished reading some of the material that's come into
my office lately," Brognola confessed. "But we'll get
to that. Go on about the leopard cult, Calvin."

"I'm hardly an expert on this subject," James
warned the others, "but I did a paper on African animism in college. As I recall, there were—or maybe I
should say *are*—different kinds of leopard cults in
Africa. Most regard the leopard as a powerful spirit of
the night. Lions don't usually hunt after dark, and
they seldom hunt alone. The leopard is the most
dreaded creature after sundown. The cultists believe
the leopard represents Paka Munga—the cat god, the
god of the night who rules the darkness."

"Including the ultimate darkness of death?" Manning ventured. "The eternal sleep?"

"Now you're getting the idea," James said with a
nod. "Anyway, the leopard cults have always been
feared in Africa because most of them believe in ritu-
alistic murder as a way of offering sacrifices to Paka
Munga. Apparently, an apprentice has to kill a member of his own family in order to join the cult. Some
of the cults are also said to engage in cannibalism."

"Oh, my God!" Brognola rasped. "According to the reports, some of the victims in Kenya have had their livers and hearts cut out."

"Jesus!" McCarter muttered. "These blokes sound worse than those Thuggees we tangled with in India a while back."

"Yeah," Manning agreed. "I think I understand why the President wants us for this mission. The Thuggees were also killing tourists and businessmen from America and Western Europe."

"Well, the situation may be similar in that respect," Brognola replied, "but at least the murders by the Thuggees in India weren't causing the kind of widespread pandemonium that's started to happen in Kenya. The shit really hit the fan this morning."

"How's that?" Encizo asked.

"A few hours after the murders of the Bowies," Hal Brognola replied, "the president of Kenya received a phone call from someone claiming responsibility for the rash of leopard-man killings. The president was told that the murders would continue unless he stepped down from office and turned Kenya over to none other than Idi Amin."

"Holy shit," James said, "that's crazy. Amin once threatened to bomb Kenya because they let the Israelis refuel there after the raid on Entebbe. Nobody has even seen Amin for years."

"I didn't say it made sense," the Fed stated, "but that's the story the president of Kenya was told. To make sure the government didn't keep a lid on the story, similar phone calls were made to the American, British, West German and French embassies in Nairobi, and probably all the others as well. Also, the country's three major newspapers were notified by the terrorists and so was the Voice of Kenya, which is the government-run radio-and-broadcasting system there. So these outrageous demands have been made public and have already had an effect on the population.''

"What sort of effect?" Encizo asked.

"Kenya has a large Christian population," the Fed answered. "It also has many followers of animism and a smaller but still significant number of Muslims. Because the murders have been the work of leopard-men, the other religious groups are blaming the animistic sects for the rash of killings. Now the claim that Idi Amin is responsible has made the Muslims targets as well, because Amin was very outspoken about being a Muslim and a radical one at that. Violence has already erupted over this business, and the government there is afraid it will get worse if somebody doesn't unravel the puzzle PDQ."

"Everybody seems to have got excited in a hurry over there," McCarter remarked. "Why are things reaching the boiling point so soon?"

"Because the Kenyans realize that their economic survival is threatened as well," Brognola explained. "Imports and exports are critical to the country. Most of its trade is with Great Britain, West Germany, Japan, Saudi Arabia and Uganda. Citizens from the first two countries have been targeted for sacrifice by the killers. That sure isn't good for business. If anti-Islamic feelings increase, Saudi Arabia won't be too eager to do business there, either. And Uganda won't stay friends with Kenya if they think there's a chance Idi Amin might take over there. Remember that during the eight years that Amin was dictator in Uganda, he had more than three hundred thousand of his own countrymen killed. Needless to say, the present government of Uganda doesn't want to see Amin in power again—especially as a hostile next-door neighbor.

"Besides," Brognola continued, "the tourist trade is threatened, and that's a major source of income in Kenya. The country is rapidly becoming a powder keg. The President, that is the President of the United States, is especially concerned because Kenya is one of the few African countries that is still on good terms with the Western nations. It's not a Communist or pro-Marxist country, either. I don't have to tell you guys that there are Soviet and Cuban advisors all over Africa. The Soviets have a firm hold on Somalia, Ethiopia, Angola and Mozambique, to name a few. We don't want them to take Kenya as well."

"I say we go to Kenya," McCarter announced. No one was surprised, because the Briton was always eager to get back into action.

"We all agree, I think," Manning stated, "but I wish we didn't have to go without Yakov. This sounds like it might be cloak-and-dagger stuff, and Katz is the expert in that field."

"He's also in a hospital bed, and blind," Brognola stated. "I'm sorry, gentlemen. I had Aaron run a computer check for somebody like Katz who could help, but there isn't anybody who comes close—except Mack Bolan, and he can't be reached. I'd have Able Team link up with you, but they're already on another mission."

"Could we get a fifth man?" Encizo suggested. "Somebody we've worked with before, like Karl Hahn or John Trent?"

"Checked that, too," the Fed answered. "Hahn isn't in Germany, and the BND isn't saying where they've assigned him. And Trent isn't in San Francisco. He went to Japan three days ago, and wherever he is, we haven't been able to find him."

"Trent's a ninja," Calvin James remarked. "Hard to say what he's doing in Japan. Of course, he's got family over there. Maybe he's just visiting them."

"I just hope he hasn't decided to start working for them," Brognola said grimly. "We came across some evidence recently that some of Trent's family might be connected to a yakuza clan."

"Trent wouldn't work for gangsters," James insisted, "American or Japanese."

"We'll discuss that later," the Fed replied. "Right now, we gotta get you guys ready for your mission. Unfortunately, it'll be just you four against whatever the hell is on the rampage in Kenya."

"Any update on Katz's condition?" Manning asked hopefully.

"Why don't you pay him a visit before you leave?" Brognola suggested. "Tell him we're all still in his corner. Okay?"

"You bet," Encizo answered, speaking for all four men as the other three nodded in unison.

5

Yakov Katzenelenbogen lay in the hospital bed with his head propped up on two pillows. The Israeli's eyes were covered with fresh bandages. Somehow, Katz seemed smaller and older to the four Phoenix Force commandos. They had never thought of their unit commander as a helpless middle-aged man gradually sliding into old age.

"You're lucky you can't see this room," McCarter joked. "It's a real dump, Yakov."

"Lucky me," Katz replied in a flat, lifeless voice.

"We spoke with Dr. Nolan," Manning said, uncertain how to talk to Katz, absurd though that seemed. Katz was one of them, a blood brother to every man on this very special team, yet he now seemed to be a stranger.

"Yeah," James added. "He told us they got all the metal shards out of your eyes, man. No punctures to the eyeball. No shrapnel damage at all . . ."

"Nolan already told me about it," Katz assured him. "He also told me the flash burns may have caused permanent damage to the retina, so don't bother telling me how lucky I am. That gets to be annoying, you know. I'm lying on my back, blind, with a stump for an arm, and people are telling me I'm lucky."

"Hal asked us to tell you he's pulling for you..." Encizo put in. "But I don't suppose you want to hear that right now."

"Not really," Katz admitted. He sat up. The blanket slid down and revealed the empty sleeve that dangled below his right elbow. "What was the outcome of the Quebec mission?"

"All the terrorists were killed except one," Manning said. "The President and the Canadian government were pleased by the results."

"I'm glad someone was," Katz commented. "Actually, I shouldn't complain. We all know the risks, and nobody knew them better than I did. Has Brognola come up with anything for you guys yet?"

"As a matter of fact he has," James answered. "We're going to Kenya—"

"Don't tell me," Katz interrupted sharply. "I'm not in the need-to-know position. Don't give me any details. You have to maintain security. And that goes for all of you. When you're in the field, try to gather as much information as possible before taking action. That's all intelligence work is—gathering information. Don't rush into things unless you have to. That's especially meant for you, David, you're too eager to charge into situations."

"I think I've heard something like that before," McCarter answered simply. "I'll try to contain myself in the future."

"You four are the best men I ever worked with," Katz told them. "The very best. This might be the end for me, but I want you to keep doing the best you can. Your work is important, and don't ever forget that."

"The end for you?" Encizo scoffed. "They haven't buried you yet, Yakov."

"Maybe they have," the Israeli replied with a weak shrug. "If not now, then in another year or two."

"That's bullshit," James growled. "I can't believe I'm hearing you talk this way, Yakov."

"I'm getting too old for this sort of thing." Katz sighed. "Maybe I had to be blind to see that. My time has come and gone. You've got a job to do. Better get to it."

"Yeah," Manning said grimly. "I guess you're right...about that, anyway."

"Let's go," McCarter agreed. "I sure as hell hope you sound more like yourself when we get back, Yakov."

"You think about what you want to do, amigo," Encizo told Katz, placing a hand on the Israeli's shoulder. "You might feel differently after a while. Don't be too eager to roll over and give up. I doubt you know how."

The Cuban walked to the door and followed Manning and McCarter into the corridor. James lingered a moment longer, wishing he knew what to say to Yakov Katzenelenbogen.

"You know," he said at last, "none of us have given up on you, Yakov. Just don't give up on yourself."

The man in the bed smiled thinly and nodded. James stepped into the hall and joined the others.

"I can't stand seeing him like that," James muttered. For the first time in years, he felt he might cry. "I had to keep telling myself that was still Katz in there."

"He's not really Katz right now," Encizo said with a shrug as they moved down the hallway. "Under the circumstances, he's got a right to be a little upset, depressed and irritable."

"True," McCarter agreed. "When a chap wakes up and discovers he's blind, it's expecting a bit much to think he should just say, 'well, not being able to see is a bit of a nuisance, but stiff-upper-lip and all that, I'll just have to adjust to it by this afternoon.' "

"That's too much to expect even from Katz," Manning said with a solemn nod. "I don't have to tell you guys what he meant by that 'maybe I'm already dead' remark. If his blindness is permanent, he won't be leading any commando teams in the future. That'll be the end of his career, and for Katz, that's his whole life."

"I don't know what I'd do if that happened to me," McCarter admitted. "Probably take it a lot worse than Katz is."

"He sounds like he's ready to give up," James said. "I realize he's been through a hell of a lot, but I just can't believe he would feel like that."

"Surprise, Calvin," Encizo replied. "Katz is human. We all feel like giving up sometimes. A lot of people quit, but Katz won't. He's been a fighter and a survivor all his life. He isn't going to change now."

"I hate to leave him like this," Manning muttered. "But we've got a mission to take care of."

"And I got a feeling that when we get in the field we're gonna really miss Katz," James remarked.

No one disagreed.

JURGEN TAUBER WATCHED the four men walk along the corridor. He had taken quite an interest in the one-armed blind man in room 123. Tauber suspected the patient was someone special. Someone he had been hoping to find for a long time.

Tauber was known at the hospital by the name of Robert Pelson. Twenty-six years old, with an athletic physique and clipped blond hair, he was attractive to most women, although he had little interest in them. Occasionally, a female was useful for relieving sexual frustrations, but women wanted to know details about the men they slept with, and Tauber had to keep his secrets if he wanted to survive, if he wanted the cause he had been raised to protect and serve to survive.

Jurgen Tauber was the son of Wolfgang-Gunther Tauber, a former member of the security staff of the Dachau concentration camp. After the Third Reich came crashing down at the end of World War II, Lieutenant Tauber had fled Europe. He had joined other Nazi war criminals in South America, including the infamous Josef Mengele, Adolf Eichmann and Klaus Barbie.

The better-known Nazi fugitives had remained in South America, but some of the more obscure war criminals had migrated to other parts of the world. Wolfgang Tauber had slipped into the United States and assumed the identity of a murdered Dutch immigrant. Known as Rutger Pelson, Wolfgang Tauber had become a naturalized U.S. citizen, had married and led a seemingly respectable middle-class existence.

But he had still been a Nazi. He had still dreamed of the day when the Third Reich would rise again and take control of the entire world. He had passed these dreams on to his son, Jurgen Tauber, who was known to the rest of the world as Robert Pelson.

Jurgen Tauber was a second-generation member of ODESSA. The clandestine worldwide Nazi network was still trying to rebuild the dreams of Adolf Hitler and the SS, financed by the enormous wealth stolen by the SS and the Gestapo during the war. Gold, diamonds, jewelry and priceless art objects had been taken, as well as millions in various currencies. ODESSA had secret bank accounts in Switzerland, South America and the Caribbean.

The Nazis in ODESSA needed all that wealth. They had to spend most of their time avoiding their enemies—especially the Israelis, who still wanted revenge for the genocide of millions of European Jews. They had to bribe government officials in South America, they had to pay for plastic surgery and the construction of hideaways in remote areas of Brazil and Paraguay. The greatest hope of ODESSA lay in its young members. Jurgen Tauber's father had died several years ago, but the son was still determined to carry on the work of the Nazi organization.

Jurgen Tauber was working as an orderly at the hospital when Yakov Katzenelenbogen arrived. He recognized that the middle-aged, one-armed patient fit the description of an enemy of ODESSA. The four men he had seen visiting the blind man also fit the description of a commando unit that had twice foiled ODESSA plans.

Katzenelenbogen was a special enemy of ODESSA, and had been for many years. ODESSA had an extensive file on the former colonel of Mossad, the Israeli intelligence agency that occasionally struck out at Nazi war criminals. When Katz was still with Mossad, he had led a strike team against an ODESSA base in southern France. Later with his four mysterious allies, Katz had ruined ODESSA schemes in West Germany and in France.

The opportunity to get revenge for the slain ODESSA members excited Tauber. The enemy had been delivered to him, blind and helpless. The situation could not be better, but Tauber did not intend to take the responsibility alone. Besides, he knew someone who had a very personal reason to want to be part of the kill.

Tauber strolled through the hall and nodded at the nurse stationed at the desk. She barely acknowledged the orderly as she was busy searching for medical records for an impatient doctor who complained that she was too slow.

Jurgen Tauber found a telephone booth near a waiting room. He slipped inside, dropped a coin into the pay phone and dialed a long-distance number. The operator told him how much his call would cost and the young Nazi fed more coins into the machine. At last, he heard the ring at the other end of the line and a familiar voice that said simply, "Hello?"

"I'm calling from the hospital," Tauber announced. "The Arlington hospital."

The man who had answered the phone knew who was calling. He did not reply for a few seconds. "Is something wrong?" he inquired.

"Someone you've wanted to meet for many years is here," Tauber explained. "Someone who knew your father in France."

"A friend of my father's?" the man asked tensely. He wanted to know if the person was a member of ODESSA or an enemy.

"An associate," Tauber replied, letting his comrade know that the person in question was an enemy. "A fairly recent associate."

The line was silent. Tauber waited, aware that Lother Zeigler understood his meaning. Lother's father, General Adolf Zeigler, had been the third highest officer in ODESSA. He had personally commanded a major operation in France, which had ended in failure. The general had killed himself rather than be taken prisoner by the enemy.

"We'll talk about this later," Lother Zeigler told him. "I'll call you at home tomorrow."

"Of course." Tauber smiled. He realized Zeigler intended to fly to Arlington as soon as possible to handle the matter in person. "Should I call your brother?"

"No," Zeigler answered. "I don't think we need to disturb him, unless you feel the matter is serious enough."

Zeigler was really asking Tauber if they needed reinforcements to deal with the enemy.

"I doubt it," Tauber replied. "After you speak with me again, you may change your mind. The decision will be yours, my friend."

"Then we'll talk again," Zeigler assured him. "Thank you for the call."

"You're welcome," Tauber said, and hung up the phone.

6

Captain Edward Mandera met the four men of Phoenix Force at the Jomo Kenyatta Airport in Nairobi. A heavy-set man with a broad dark face, Mandera wore sunglasses with very dark lenses, although the morning sky was not especially bright. Most officers in law enforcement or in the military in African nations wear such glasses to conceal expressions of their eyes, and thus to avoid revealing their thoughts.

Kenya is a one-party republic, not a dictatorship but not a democracy, either. KANU, the Kenya African National Union, is the only legal political party in Kenya.

This was something of an advantage for Phoenix Force. The President of the United States had asked the government of Kenya to allow an American military transport plane to land and to waive customs and immigration procedures for the special four-man team aboard the craft. He had also asked the Kenyans to assist the visitors in their efforts to stamp out the terrorism that had rocked the African republic. The government agreed eagerly and prepared for the arrival of Phoenix Force. There was no need for red tape or confrontations with public agencies. The central government said "do it" and it was done.

Captain Mandera introduced himself to Phoenix Force and showed them his identification as an officer in the Kenyan National Security Service. The four visitors in turn showed Mandera their passports. The African realized this was just a gesture. Phoenix Force was using phony identification with their current cover names, and Mandera knew it.

They said little as they removed their aluminum suitcases and long rifle cases from the luggage hold of the plane. Mandera told them he had a car waiting, and the five men passed through the airport to the Cadillac limousine parked at the curb, a number of taxicabs lined up behind it. Tiny flags were mounted above the headlights of the limo—the national flag of Kenya, with red, green and black bands, and a shield with crossed spears in the center.

"Government car?" Manning inquired, although he knew that it was.

"Is that all right?" Mandera asked as he helped them put the luggage in the vehicle. They kept most of the baggage with them and put only the rifle cases in the trunk.

"We'll need something less conspicuous later," Encizo told the security officer. "You know the driver?"

"Sergeant Wafula Ngong," Captain Mandera introduced the man behind the steering wheel. "Very trustworthy. Wafula is a former Nairobi police officer and knows the city well.''

Sergeant Ngong greeted the men with a broad grin. He appeared to be in his mid-thirties, and also wore the dark glasses of a security man who understands the realities of African politics.

''The sergeant is very good at his job, and he speaks English, Swahili, Kikuyu and Arabic,'' the captain stated. ''This may prove useful for you. Yes?''

''I also speak a little Luo,'' the driver added as he tugged the brim of his cloth cap over the rim of his glasses. ''Although most Luo speak Swahili or English these days.''

Everyone climbed into the limo, and it pulled away from the curb. The men of Phoenix Force noticed that the thick glass was tinted to keep outsiders from peering into the car and was also shatter-resistant. The limo appeared to be semiarmored.

''We've got a pretty good idea about the problem here,'' Calvin James began as he unbuttoned his white linen suit jacket, exposing the leather strap of a shoulder holster under the lapel. ''Do you have anything new for us?''

''Not much, I'm afraid,'' the African replied with a sigh. ''The most recent murder victims, the Bowies, were probably set up—I think that's the expression—by a desk clerk at the hotel they were staying at. The man disappeared after they were killed. The name he used when he was employed by the hotel proved to be false. We have no knowledge of his true identity or whom he may have been associated with."

"The murders seem to be the work of so-called leopard-men," Manning remarked. "Is there any evidence to either confirm or disprove this?"

"The killings were certainly done in that fashion," Mandera answered. "But we don't know if the killers are really members of a leopard cult, or imitators using that technique of homicide."

"I don't think a real leopard cult is involved," Sergeant Ngong commented as he steered the limo around a slower-moving vehicle.

"Why not?" James asked.

"Because the leopard cults never single out whites for targets," Ngong answered. "And they never get involved in politics. Why should they? They don't care about the issues of the day. As long as they can worship Paka Munga and occasionally hunt like a leopard so they can be one with the god of the night, they don't care who's in charge of the government."

"I assume 'hunting like a leopard' is illegal in Kenya," Encizo remarked. "Maybe the leopard-men figured they could hunt better with a different government. They might think the present one gets in the way of their religion."

"Pretty weird theory," Ngong mused.

"People who tear apart other people as human sacrifices to a cat god are a little weird, too," McCarter stated. "And don't give me any lectures about putting down animism. The right of anybody to practice their religion ends when they start harming innocent people."

"Oh, I agree," Ngong assured him. "But I still don't think real leopard-men are involved. The human victims they kill usually live in remote, rather backward villages. I investigated a couple of cases like that, and never caught the killers. By the time the police found out about the killings, the trail was already cold. Besides, uneducated peasants are more apt to believe the leopard-men have magic powers, and they're less willing to cooperate with the authorities. Many will simply accept the death of a victim of a leopard-man as fate, or as being from natural causes."

"Murder by natural causes?" Encizo inquired.

"To some people," Ngong replied. "Sort of like lightning bolts or earthquakes. If someone is killed by a real leopard or a snakebite or a crocodile, you wouldn't call it murder. Well, some of the more superstitious tribesmen believe the leopard-men can really transform themselves into leopards."

"You mean like werewolves or something?" McCarter asked.

"Exactly," Ngong confirmed. "They believe in magic, and the leopard-men claim to have the magic of Paka Munga. In fact, the leopard-men themselves seem to believe this. They dress up in leopard skins, you know. They snarl and roar like leopards. They run on all fours and sometimes even eat parts of their victims. On a dark night, a frightened peasant could easily mistake a leopard-man for a big cat, or worse, for a leopard that's part human. Big magic.''

"Okay," Manning began, "I think it's pretty unlikely that the leopard cults got together to force the current government to let them have all of Kenya on their menu. How about the possibility that Idi Amin really *is* behind this mess?''

"That's absurd," Mandera answered. "Amin would be insane to try something like that."

"Amin qualifies," McCarter reminded the African. "Amin wanted to erect a statue of Adolf Hitler in the center of Kampala. He had thousands of people killed for reasons even he couldn't make sense of. Amin isn't playing with a full deck, mate. According to a file on Amin, when he was a sergeant major in the British army in the days when Uganda was still a colony, he was treated for syphilis, which may or may not have caused brain damage."

"At least that would explain his excesses," Encizo said with a shrug. "But the big question is whether or not the madman of Uganda could get enough support to try something like this."

"The last I heard of Idi Amin," Mandera remarked, "he fled Uganda in 1979, after Tanzanian troops seized control of Kampala. He wound up in Saudi Arabia, and as far as I know he's still there, unless the Saudis decided to get rid of the louse. I doubt that he could rally any support in Kenya, unless it might be from some of the more radical Muslim groups."

"Are there many radical Muslim groups in Kenya?" James inquired.

"Not really," Mandera said. "But there are some, notably the Islamic Equality Movement, which we've got under surveillance. But I think the terrorists are probably Tanzanians, possibly working for the KGB."

"I know Kenya and Tanzania haven't always gotten along very well," James said. "But I didn't realize there was any current hostility between your country and Tanzania."

"Tanzania is a socialist dictatorship," Mandera said with contempt. "That's a half step away from communism."

"Tanzania doesn't seem to be in the Soviet camp," Manning remarked. "Their government trades with the West—the United States, Great Britain, Japan, Italy. I wasn't aware that the Tanzanians did much business with the Communists."

"And the socialism in Tanzania doesn't have much in common with Soviet-style communism," James added. "I think President Nyerere has described it as a variation of the old commune-type village life."

"That's true," Ngong remarked. "He calls it *ujamaa*—Swahili for 'the way of the family.'"

Mandera looked disapprovingly at the sergeant. "I wouldn't think you men would approve of socialism," he said to Phoenix Force.

"I wouldn't say we approve," Manning answered, "but Tanzania isn't Angola or Mozambique. There aren't any Cuban or Soviet advisors there. Frankly, if a government isn't trying to muscle into other nations and isn't notably abusive to its own people, then it's affairs are nobody else's business. Back in the late seventies, Uganda, under Idi Amin, declared war on Tanzania. Not the other way around. The Tanzanians acted in self-defense. They more or less won the war, but they didn't claim conquest and they withdrew their troops from Uganda. That suggests Tanzania isn't interested in conquest.''

"I still suspect the Tanzanians are involved in these murders," Mandera insisted. "Perhaps some radical terrorists connected with the KGB. I trust you aren't going to defend the Soviet KGB, too.''

"Would you feel better if we criticized Tanzania?" McCarter asked. "Fine with me. It's a bloody one-party republic, so-called that is, which means it doesn't have free elections since there's nothing to choose between. How's that, mate?''

Mandera glared at the Briton. McCarter's description also fit Kenya perfectly. Manning quickly smoothed things over.

"KGB involvement in terrorist groups is something we've come up against several times in the past," he declared. "How active is the KGB in Kenya?''

"We've got them here," Mandera confirmed. "But basically they're just gathering general intelligence about the country and spying on the other embassies here in Nairobi. Of course, Ethiopia borders us on the north. They have a Communist dictatorship with Soviet ties ... no argument on that?''

"None," Encizo assured him. "Please go on."

"Well, the Ethiopian government is disunited," Mandera stated. "They're not well enough organized to conduct any subversive acts here in Kenya, but they might be able to send in trained terrorists to do some dirty work for the KGB. God knows the Ethiopian leaders are savage enough to hire people to tear others to pieces. I know you Americans have delivered millions of dollars' worth of food and other aid to Ethiopia, but don't think they're grateful."

"I'm sure the people who received the help are," James stated.

"Well, to get back to what you people are here for," Mandera remarked, "I really don't think that Ethiopians are involved in the murders here in Kenya. The Ethiopian government is preoccupied with the civil war with the province of Eritrea, which is going into its twenty-fifth year."

"But the KGB could be mixed up in it," Manning mused, gazing out the window at Government Road, which cut through the heart of downtown Nairobi. A well-maintained four-lane highway with palm trees planted along the median strips, it looked right out of Southern California.

"How bad is the conflict between the religious factions within Kenya?" Encizo asked. "We understand the Muslims and the animist groups are being blamed for the murders by a lot of people here."

"There haven't been any full-scale riots or bloodshed, but we know of some pretty nasty beatings,"

Mandera replied. "And a lynch party did hang one fellow they claimed was involved with a leopard cult. He had a couple of leopard skins in his home, true, but he also had horns and antelope skins and a zebra head mounted on a plaque. We think he was probably a poacher."

"No loss," Ngong commented. "I think he deserved to hang."

"Maybe so," Mandera allowed. "But the situation threatens to get worse. Usually we Kenyans get along pretty well. Some of us Christians even have friends who are Muslims or animists."

"You're not my friend, Captain," Ngong said, laughing, "you're my commanding officer."

"I didn't say I was talking about myself," Mandera told him, then continued to make his point. "There are always zealots who see other religions as evil, and they're usually Christians and Muslims, I'm sorry to say. Not many, you understand, but they're there and they're stirring up trouble. The animist groups are especially vulnerable, because both Christians and Muslims regard them as godless heathens in league with the devil. If we could disprove the story about Idi Amin being involved in this, it would take the pressure off the Muslim community, but because of the leopard-man style of the killings, the followers of the old religions will continue to be targets for overzealous members of the other faiths until the whole matter is resolved."

"Shit," James muttered sourly. "We don't have any idea where to begin. I wish Katz was here."

The other members of Phoenix Force felt the same way.

"Let's get settled in," Manning suggested. "Once we've unpacked and had something to eat, we'll be in better shape to decide what to do next."

"Maybe we should get a Ouija board," McCarter said.

7

Chou Ziyang smiled as he bowed formally to the two black men at either side of the mat. Just over five feet six, the slender Chinese seemed relaxed as he raised his arms in the praying mantis position, wrists bent and fingers arched. His feet shifted to a horse stance as he waited for his opponents to make the first move.

The black men were both larger and more muscular than Chou, but they had sparred with the Asian before and did not underestimate him. In fact, Chou had beaten the hell out of them on several occasions. Today he had invited them both to take him on at the same time. They were too proud to refuse the challenge and hoped finally to get the better of the arrogant Chinese.

The first opponent attacked, swinging his arms up in an elaborate feint as he swung a kick at Chou's groin. A palm slap deflected the black man's shin before his foot could reach its intended target. Chou blocked a punch with his forearm and thrust the stiffened fingers of his other hand into the breastbone of his opponent. The African groaned and staggered backward, gasping for air.

The second opponent closed in from Chou's right, and swung a fist at the Asian's sleek head. Chou jumped aside and avoided the punch, then swiftly seized the other man's wrist and elbow. Chou turned sharply and applied pressure to lock his opponent's arm.

"Not good enough, comrade," he murmured in Swahili as he pulled with one arm and pushed with the other.

The African was thrown head over heels to the mat. As he tumbled across the floor, the first African launched a high roundhouse kick at the Asian's head. Chou's hands rose to snare his opponent's ankle, then turned slightly and dropped to one knee. The black man was thrown off balance and flew across the room to crash into the wall.

The second African rose from the floor and charged, fists clenched in anger. Chou suddenly leaped into the air and slashed a crescent kick to the man's face. His slipper-shod foot slammed into the black's cheekbone and sent him sprawling on the mat. Chou landed nimbly on his feet in a horse stance and noticed that Li Yuann had entered the *kwoon*.

"*Di xiong...*" Li began urgently.

"*Deng yi...*" Chou replied sharply. He noticed his first opponent had launched himself at him once more, attacking from behind.

Chou delivered a swift back-kick to the man's midsection. The African doubled up with a gasp. Chou whipped a back fist to the man's face, immediately followed by a blow with the heel of his other hand, which smashed the black's mouth. Chou lashed the side of his hand under the African's heart, and the man collapsed in a daze, vomiting on the mat.

"Now we may talk, Comrade Li," Chou declared. He barely glanced at the pair of vanquished opponents as he walked calmly away from them, seeming unconcerned that they might have been injured during the training exercise.

"Your *chuan shu* skills are as impressive as ever, comrade," Li told him. "Personally, I have more faith in a good firearm."

"Martial arts training is mostly discipline," Chou said proudly. "Chairman Mao wrote much about the importance of discipline."

"He also said 'All power comes from the barrel of a gun,'" Li said with a smile.

"Hau," Chou replied. "But Mao also warned, 'The Party commands the gun, but the gun must never be allowed to command the Party.' Besides, firearms can jam and run out of ammo. Your body is the only weapon you can always rely on."

"As Lin Piao once said, 'Comrade Mao is the greatest Marxist-Leninist of our era,'" Li said with heartfelt sincerity.

"'And he brought it to a higher and completely new stage,'" Chou added with equal reverence.

The two Chinese quoted the works of Mao as devoutly as a devout Christian might quote the Bible. Indeed the *Quotations from Chairman Mao Tse-tung,* often called The Little Red Book, was their scripture. They had embraced the new faith twenty years ago and had never strayed from the path of truth and enlightenment according to Chairman Mao.

Chou and Li had been members of Mao's Red Guard, youthful zealots who were brainwashed by the nonstop propaganda campaigns in China during the 1960s. Thousands of young Maoists had marched through the streets of Peking, chanting and waving banners, praising Mao as if he were a god, and following his commandments with blind devotion.

Communism was opposed to religion, so the Red Guard considered it their sacred duty to beat up or kill those who still practiced the ancient religions of Taoism, Confucianism and Buddhism.

The Red Guard also destroyed temples and thousands of wonderful works of cultural value that could never be replaced. Literature was destroyed for the same reason. These acts were not just atrocities against living people—although Mao Tse-tung also claimed the greatest body count in the history of genocide, slaughtering at least seventy million people—they were crimes against the very spirit of mankind.

After Mao's death, the worship of his Little Red Book came to an end. China established new relations with the West and dismantled many communal farms and state-owned businesses and shops. Political prisoners were released. Most Chinese welcomed the changes.

The so-called Gang of Four were tried and convicted of killing nearly thirty-five thousand people during the Cultural Revolution and unjustly persecuting hundreds of thousands of others. The reign of Mao Tse-tung truly ended.

But Chou and Li could not accept these developments.

Mao was still their god, and The Little Red Book was still their holy scripture.

In 1976, when the political tides in China turned against the memory of Mao Tse-tung, Chou and Li and a few other former Red Guard fanatics fled the country. Mao had urged his followers to "give active support to the national independence and liberation movement in countries in Asia, Africa and Latin America," that is, to overthrow any foreign government that did not endorse a Marxist-Leninist philosophy.

Chou and Li settled in Kenya. They had spent ten years planning their revolution and preparing for the time to take action against the imperialist enemies. At last that time had come, and the first phase had been carried out successfully.

"You seemed eager to speak with me, comrade," Chou said, as he and Li walked the long corridor of adobe brick walls and stone floors. "Is something wrong?"

"On the contrary, Comrade Chou," Li replied with a sly smile. "The news is most encouraging. The religious idiots are busy blaming each other. They're truly terrified of losing the support of the powers of the West.''

''These African nations are too weak to survive on their own,'' Chou stated, speaking in Chinese to be certain none of the Africans working at the plantation overheard them. ''Blacks have not channeled their intelligence into productive enterprises. That's why the whites took over the countries of Africa. After the Europeans leave, black Africans butcher each other until the Russians move in.''

''The Russians may move into Kenya if we're not careful,'' Li warned. ''Do you think we should move to the next phase?''

''That may be rushing things, comrade.'' Chou frowned. ''Chairman Mao warned that plans must be scrutinized carefully to make certain they are really well founded. We mustn't become careless because we are too eager.''

''Mao also said 'Communists should be practical as well as farsighted,''' Li insisted. ''The practical thing to do is to guard against the Soviets moving in before we can secure a hold on Kenya.''

''Perhaps you're right,'' Chou stated as he peered out a window.

On the parade field below several Africans were attacking dummies made of bamboo and straw. The men pounced on the dummies, and with the steel claws strapped to their hands they tore at the dummies' ''throats'' and clawed into their bellies and faces.

"What a splendid example of Mao's theories of military training," Chou said with satisfaction. "The officer trains the soldier, and when the soldier has more experience as a fighter, the soldier trains the officer, until at last the soldier teaches the soldier because they are all equal and there is no need of rank."

"Remember Mao's statement about training, that special emphasis be placed on night operations?" Li said reverently. "It is as if Mao has guided our every move, Comrade."

"He has," Chou replied. "This victory will be as much Chairman Mao's victory as ours. We are using his methods to defeat the reactionaries. Soon they will strike out at each other, forcing the authorities to resort to drastic measures to control them. Soon the police and the military will be recognized as the enemies of the people."

"Then the people will rise up against their real enemy—the state that oppresses them," Li added. "And in the chaos that follows, we shall bring them salvation in the form of Maoist communism—that is, if the Soviets don't get in ahead of us."

"Do you think that really is a possibility?" Chou asked with a weary sigh.

"During the sixties Chinese influence in the Congo and Mozambique was very great," Li reminded him. "But the Soviets forced our advisors out and seized control. We can't risk that happening again here."

"Very well," Chou agreed reluctantly. "We'll go ahead with the second phase of our plan."

8

Yakov Katzenelenbogen heard the door to his hospital room open. Light footsteps moved across the floor, and nylon rustled against nylon. A faint floral scent teased his nostrils.

"Who are you?" he demanded, bracing himself on his elbows to sit up in the bed.

"I'm Dr. Kyler," a woman's voice announced cheerfully, "Julia Kyler. I was one of the team who operated on you the other day. How are you feeling?"

"Depressed," he growled. "How else would I feel, Doctor?"

"I can understand that," Dr. Kyler replied as she drew closer. "But you have a very good chance of recovering your eyesight, Mr.... How's this name pronounced anyway?"

"I don't care how you pronounce it," Katz told her. "Is the cheering-up business finished now?"

"Oh, yeah," she answered. "Would you like to be left alone to feel sorry for yourself in private? I don't like people watching when I snivel and pout, either."

"Right," Katz said, with an edge in his voice. "So just leave me alone."

"You know your last name really is impossible." She sighed. Katz heard her flip through some papers. "Guess I'll have to call you Yakov. That means you'll have permission to call me Julia. I don't think it's fair for doctors to call their patients by their first names and expect the patients to address them by their titles."

"I'm about to call you something else," Katz said, annoyed. "I'd really like to be left alone, Doctor."

"Don't worry," she assured him. "I'll be going soon. You know, there are two Justice Department agents stationed outside your door. I guess you're some sort of government man. Frankly, you surprise me. You've obviously been injured more than once before. You lost your right arm some time ago, but a lot of the other scars are more recent. In general, you're in good physical shape—"

"I'm blind and you say I'm in good shape?" Katz chuckled. "What kind of doctor are you?"

"A damn good one," Julia Kyler replied. "My point is, I would have guessed you to be the sort of man who wouldn't be willing to lie down and give up until he was brain-dead."

"Maybe I am brain-dead," he shot back.

"You've almost got me convinced," she answered.

"You want me to count my blessings, or what?"

"I know people with less to be thankful for than you have."

"Really?" Katz said sharply. "How many blind, one-armed middle-aged men do you know, Doctor?"

"I have patients who are almost totally paralyzed," the doctor told him. "They can't move their limbs, they can't move their heads very well and they defecate into bags and have to depend on others to take care of the waste. Want to trade places with them?"

"Are you finished?" Katz said with a sigh.

"Not quite," Dr. Kyler continued. "I've got other patients who've suffered brain damage. They can't remember how to walk or to talk clearly. They can't remember anything a minute after they learn it. They can't read a child's storybook because they can't even remember what the alphabet is. But you could get out of the bed and walk if you'd get off your ass, Yakov."

"What for?" Katz demanded. "So I can stagger around in the dark? Don't you understand? Everything is dark to me."

"Including your future?"

"Especially my future," Katz said softly.

"I do feel sorry for you," she said gently. "But I've got other things to do and I've got patients who aren't already a lost cause. Let me know if you decide you want to live."

"You don't understand," Katz said, shaking his head.

"Maybe I could if you told me, Yakov."

"I'm being forced to face something I prayed would never happen," he said in an unsteady voice.

"Blindness?"

"Retirement," Katz explained.

"You're more upset by that than blindness?" Dr. Kyler asked with surprise. "You must have one hell of a job, Yakov."

"Oh, yes." He smiled. "Quite a job."

"I don't suppose you can tell me about it?"

"I'm afraid not."

"That's what I figured. I guess that's why the untouchables are outside your door. Look, Yakov..."

"I wish I could," he said, surprised that he was able to joke about his blindness.

"Okay, listen instead." She laughed in response. "You have an excellent chance of recovering your eyesight, but even if that doesn't happen, you really can do other things with your life. You're still in good health and you're reasonably attractive."

"Thank you," Yakov said.

"Don't let it go to your head," she warned. "I bet you're even above average intelligence, although you haven't sounded much like it so far."

"Self-pity really isn't all that rewarding." Katz's brow creased with a frown. "I think I've had enough of it."

Katz climbed out of bed, feeling his way along the bedside counter with his fingers. Julia Kyler placed a hand on his shoulder.

"Take my arm and I'll guide you over to the bathroom," she told him instinctively.

"Thank you," Katz replied, finding the crook of her arm. "It's over there, isn't it?" Katz turned his head toward the bathroom.

"Very good," Dr. Kyler said with surprise. "How did you know?"

"I've heard the water running and the fan humming in that direction."

"Glad to see you're using your other senses," Dr. Kyler remarked. "Your eyes will be bandaged for a few more days. The waiting will be easier if you spend the time trying to adjust to blindness."

"Just in case it's permanent?" Katz inquired as he felt the doorway with the edge of his foot.

"Are you a realist, Yakov?" the doctor asked, opening the bathroom door for him. She guided Katz to the sink, and placed his hand on the porcelain rim.

"I try to be," he answered. "The trouble is that realism leans more toward pessimism than optimism. There's always a fifty-fifty chance that something will go wrong."

"And a fifty-fifty chance that it won't," she countered.

"The toilet is to the left?" he asked.

"Yes," Dr. Kyler confirmed. "You can find your way back all right?"

"And I can manage to use the toilet by myself, too," he said, chuckling. "I think I can find where everything is. There is a chance that I'll be blind for the rest of my life, isn't there?"

"Fifty-fifty," she answered. "Those are the odds, pessimist."

"The same as always." Katz smiled, then added, "I wonder if you could see about getting my prosthesis brought to me. I think I'd like to have my other arm back."

"We can get you *a* prosthesis," she assured him. "I can't promise it'll be the one you had in Canada. I don't think it arrived with you here in Arlington."

"No, I don't suppose it did," Katz agreed. He recalled that he had been wearing a prosthetic arm with a .22 caliber pistol built into the "hand." The other members of Phoenix Force would have taken the device to avoid creating more suspicion about Katz's role in Quebec. "Another good prosthesis would be nice."

"I'll see what I can do for you," the doctor said. "I can get you a cane, too, if you like. You can use it to probe in front of you so you can walk without tripping."

"Fine," Katz said. "But I'd like a good hardwood cane. Walnut or rock maple. I don't know what they make those white canes of, but I want something sturdy."

"Plan to bash somebody over the head?" she asked, only half joking.

"You never know," he said. "I might decide to bash the hospital administrator when I get the bill."

"I'll take care of it," Dr. Kyler promised. "You just keep doing as you're doing now and you'll be fine."

9

Two Land Rovers pulled into the settlement at the outskirts of the city of Kitui. The encampment was small, just a ring of canvas tents. A couple of battered old trucks were parked to one side of the tents, and a small herd of goats grazed nearby. A group of robed tribesmen with *keffiyehs*, the traditional Arab headdress, watched the vehicles approach. Two of the men held old British Enfield rifles at port arms.

"I've seen friendlier greetings," Gary Manning muttered as the Land Rover he was riding in came to a halt.

"I've seen worse, too," Calvin James commented from the back seat. "At least they aren't *pointing* the guns at us."

"These are tough customers," Sergeant Ngong warned as he got out from behind the steering wheel of the lead vehicle. "They call themselves *Zenji*...."

"The story you told us about them wasn't very encouraging," James commented.

Zenji was an old Arab term for black people, a term used with respect. The *Zenji* states were once separate powers within Kenya, ruled by Arab traders who had settled in Malindi and Mombasa. The Arab influence gradually subsided in Kenya, but a handful of Arabs remained.

The Zenji were proud of the Muslim traditions handed down by their ancestors. Some of the Zenji were part Arab, but most were black Africans descended from converts to Islam in the old Arab states. They had been persecuted by various groups throughout Kenya's history and were therefore suspicious, clannish and sometimes hostile to outsiders who meddled in their affairs. The Zenji could be dangerous enemies.

"Assalamo alaykum." Sergeant Ngong greeted the Zenji in Arabic as he stepped from the jeep.

"Ow-zen ay?" one of the tribesmen demanded in a gruff tone.

"How are they responding, Sergeant?" Captain Mandera inquired as he emerged from the other Land Rover with David McCarter and Rafael Encizo.

"They want to know what we want," Ngong answered, "and they don't seem very happy to have us here."

"We are not happy," a tall Zenji announced as he marched toward the Phoenix Force group. The green scarf of his *keffiyeh* covered his face, except for the sand-colored eyes peering over the top.

"Maybe we came to the wrong place," McCarter commented, cocking back his khaki beret with a fingertip. "One of the reasons I've enjoyed working with

Muslims in the past was their custom of good manners."

"We would not come to see you without invitation," the Zenji stated as he pulled the scarf from his face. His high cheekbones and hawk nose suggested Semitic ancestry. "And you don't look like you're here for a social call."

He examined the four Phoenix commandos and the two security officials. The six men were dressed in khaki bush shirts and trousers and paratrooper boots. They carried pistols on their hips, and McCarter and Encizo also carried machine pistols, which hung from long shoulder straps within easy reach.

"National Security Service," Mandera announced, reaching for his identification.

The two Zenji with rifles pointed their weapons at Mandera. He raised his hands to shoulder level, jerking his arms upward as if abruptly pulled by invisible strings. Sergeant Ngong also raised his hands, but the four Phoenix Force professionals did not bat an eye. McCarter and Encizo stepped behind James and Manning so the Zenji could not see them grab the pistol grips of their subguns.

"If you guys start shooting you're going to lose," Manning warned, folding his arms on his chest. "Put the guns down."

"The situation isn't as one-sided as you might think," the Zenji leader declared as he raised his left hand. His robe fell open, revealing the butt of an old Webley revolver thrust in his silk sash.

Five more Zenji emerged from the surrounding tents. Two carried Enfields, another held a World War II German MP-40 Schmeisser in his fists. A short Zenji, dressed in a flowing striped robe two sizes too large for his diminutive frame, carried a Luger P-08 pistol with a drum magazine attached to the butt. The fifth man was a huge, very dark-skinned African with thick muscles that bulged from his naked arms and chest. He held a short-barreled double-bore shotgun in his massive fists.

"I think you should put down your weapons now," the Zenji leader said confidently.

"Why?" James asked calmly. "The odds are just about even now. We'll probably all get killed, but everybody dies sooner or later."

"I am prepared to meet Allah's judgment," the Zenji chief declared, placing his right hand on the butt of his Webley revolver.

"I hope all your people feel the same way," Encizo commented. "Because the Kenyan government will come down hard on the Zenji if we get killed here. You see, we came to talk to you folks about the terrorist murders of Americans and Europeans that have been taking place in Kenya. You heard about that, fella?"

"My people have nothing to do with that," the chief insisted.

"Nobody's going to believe that if we get killed here today," James told him. "Aren't you Mohammed Wajir, the leader of the Islamic Equality Movement?"

"That is true," the Zenji chief admitted. "But I have broken no laws. Our movement seeks only justice in Kenya, for Muslims as well as others."

"Well," McCarter said firmly, "a few people figure you blokes might be responsible for the murders we're talking about. After we all shoot each other, the fellow who takes your place as leader of the Islamic Equality Movement will have a hard time convincing anyone that your people are innocent. But, what the hell, that'll be his problem. All you'll have to worry about is how Allah will regard the fact you got a lot of people, including yourself, killed for a pretty stupid reason."

"You brought those guns for a discussion?" Wajir asked suspiciously.

"We were told your people are armed and dangerous," Manning explained. "That doesn't mean you're bad. We're armed and dangerous, too, but we're really wonderful guys when you get to know us. So let's calm down and discuss this in a civilized manner."

"Very well," Wajir agreed. He barked a curt order in Arabic. The Zenji gunmen reluctantly lowered their weapons.

"Good," James commented. "We can all relax a little. Now, your group has been accused of being involved in violent confrontations with some Christian groups and with some of the tribes that follow the old traditions and the old animistic religions."

"Heathen religions," Wajir answered with contempt. "Even the Christians agree that those spirit worshipers are evil and worship false gods."

"I'm a Christian and I don't think they're evil," Mandera stated. "Misguided, perhaps, but evil requires conscious will to commit an act one knows to be wrong."

"Some might say your efforts to convert the Masai cattle herders to Islam were wrong," Sergeant Ngong added.

"Christian missionaries have also tried to convert those backward tribes," the Zenji leader complained. "You see nothing wrong in that?"

"Wait a minute," Manning put in. "We're not here to debate religion. But we understand a couple of the Masai tribesmen were killed in a fight with some of the members of your movement."

"That was very unfortunate," Wajir said tensely. "But those members were expelled from our group and stood trial for their crimes. My own brother was killed two years ago during a confrontation with a group of Christian fanatics. None of those Christians were found guilty of murder. Is that just?"

"No, it isn't," James agreed. "But we're not here to discuss past injustices, except for the murders of Americans and Europeans that have happened recently."

"So you're an American?" Wajir smiled thinly at Calvin James. "You American blacks come to Africa and say how beautiful the 'motherland' is. You overlook injustice and corruption in black African governments because you don't want these realities to cloud your image of noble Africa, the land of your ancestors—''

"Hey, man," James interrupted sharply. "I'm here on business, so stuff that jive crap. If I was trying to find my roots, I wouldn't be talking to a guy like you. Now, do you know anything about these murders or not? Don't dick us around anymore, just answer us."

"Of course I know nothing about such crimes," Wajir snapped. "But I don't suppose you believe me."

"You folks don't like Americans much, do you?" Manning commented. "I hear you folks protested against Kenya continuing foreign relations with the United States. You assembled in front of the U.S. embassy and chanted 'Yankee go home' and other anti-American slogans."

"Amerika." The big Zenji without a shirt spit out the word with contempt and then literally spit at Manning's feet. He placed his shotgun on the ground and hissed something in rapid Arabic.

"What's his problem?" James asked, glaring at the muscle-bound Zenji tribesman.

"He wants to fight," Wajir replied. "Abu is a very strong wrestler, but nobody here will give him any practice. He often breaks men's bones without meaning to do them harm. If he fought in earnest, he might indeed kill his opponent."

"Maybe he should try a tranquilizer," McCarter suggested. "Now, I think we were talking about your group's attitude to Americans."

"We don't like them, or you British for that matter," Wajir admitted. "You've tried to force Western customs and Christianity on Africans, just as the Soviets try to force communism down our throats."

"Then you also protested in front of the Soviet embassy?" Encizo inquired. "Funny thing that there's nothing on file about that."

"We didn't protest at the Soviet embassy for a very good reason," Wajir answered angrily. "The Kenyan government troops attacked us when we demonstrated in front of the American building. Several of our people were severely beaten by the soldiers. It seemed pointless to go through that again to protest Soviet communism."

"He might be telling the truth," Mandera stated. "The demonstrations against the U.S. were in September of 1982, a month after the police had crushed an attempted rebellion against the central government. The troops may have overreacted when they broke up the Islamic Equality Movement demonstrations at the American embassy. But considering what happened during the attempted overthrow of the Kenya African National Union government, that is understandable."

"A hundred and forty-five people were killed during the attempted coup," Sergeant Ngong told the men of Phoenix Force. "Several hundred others were injured."

Mandera threw a dagger stare at Ngong. He did not appreciate the sergeant discussing details of the uprising in front of the others. Phoenix Force, however, was already familiar with the incident, although government repression in Kenya received far less American media coverage than apartheid in South Africa. They also knew that the KANU ruling party had closed most of the universities because so many students had supported the rebellion, or at least had objected to the parliament's unanimous decision in 1982 to make the Kenya African National Union the only legal political party.

So, Kenya was not a utopia, but neither was anyplace else. Kenya was still pro-Western and granted its people more rights and privileges than many African countries. Besides, Phoenix Force was in Kenya for a mission, not to seek out political shortcomings or reform government policies.

Abu, the big Zenji with all the muscles, pointed at Manning and poked himself in the chest with the other hand. He smiled and said something in Arabic. Mohammed Wajir shook his head.

"It seems Abu has chosen you for his opponent," the Zenji chief told Manning. "He says you look strong enough to give him a little exercise before he breaks you in half."

"I don't intend to play games with him," Manning replied, barely glancing at Abu. "Does the Islamic

Equality Movement have any connection with Idi Amin?''

"The former president of Uganda?" Wajir shook his head, and his tone of voice revealed his surprise at the question. "That's absurd."

"So everybody tells us," James answered. "But some folks think it's possible."

"Amin is a *Hadj*," David McCarter remarked. "He made the holy pilgrimage to Mecca. That must earn him some respect among other Muslims."

"I don't even know if Idi Amin is still alive," Wajir insisted. "Just because Amin is a Muslim, even a *Hadj*, we would not necessarily give him shelter and aid. Amin harmed the image of the African Islamic movement. Given the opportunity, I might just shoot the bastard myself."

Wajir had barely ended his sentence when Abu suddenly lunged forward toward Gary Manning, both arms extended. The Canadian quickly grabbed Abu's right wrist and turned sharply, increasing the Zenji's forward momentum and swinging him off balance. Abu hurtled out of control and slammed into the hood of one of the Land Rovers.

The big Zenji bounced off the vehicle and immediately launched a kick for Manning's crotch. The Phoenix pro blocked the attack with crossed forearms and shoved the African's leg aside. He quickly hooked his left fist to Abu's kidney and rammed a right under the guy's ribs.

Abu grunted and slashed a hard backhand stroke to Manning's face. The Canadian's head snapped back from the force of the blow, and Abu grabbed Manning's shoulders. A big knee slammed into the Phoenix pro's belly, and Abu wrapped an arm around the Canadian's neck to apply a front headlock.

Manning did not waste time trying to pry apart the African's grip. He pulled on the crook of his opponent's elbow with one hand to ease the pressure of the hold and reached the other hand between Zenji's legs. Manning grabbed Abu's testicles, squeezed hard and twisted his wrist.

Abu howled in agony and released Manning. The brawny Phoenix fighter shoved a shoulder into his opponent's abdomen and scooped up the man's legs to toss him across his back. Then Manning stood and sent Abu hurtling to the ground. Several Zenji tribesmen gasped in surprise and glanced at the other Phoenix Force teammates who stood watching the fight. They did not try to assist, aware that this was a one-on-one contest. To interfere would cause Phoenix Force to lose face in front of Wajir's people. Besides, they knew Manning would not want them to get involved in the battle unless other Zenji jumped into the fight first.

"Had enough?" Manning asked as he watched Abu climb to his feet.

The big African massaged his bruised testicles and glared at Manning. Rage filled his eyes as he lunged wildly at the Canadian. The Phoenix fighter sidestepped to avoid the charge, but Abu managed to swing an arm around his waist. The Zenji swiftly locked the fingers of both hands at the small of Manning's back and applied a powerful bear hug.

The muscular African squeezed hard, trying to crush Manning's torso in the viselike grip. Manning gasped as the pressure on his kidneys increased and his lungs struggled for air. Abu lifted Manning's feet off the ground as he continued to squeeze with all his considerable might.

Manning swatted his open palms across Abu's ears. The African bellowed in pain when an eardrum burst, but he held on. Manning bent an elbow and smashed a front-stroke to the side of the Zenji's head. Abu fell to one knee, and his grip began to slip.

Gary Manning slammed his knee under his opponent's jaw. Abu's head recoiled as if it had been struck by a bullet. He crashed unconscious to the ground, arms flung wide apart. The brutal contest ended, Manning stepped away from the vanquished foe, breathing heavily from the exertion and stress.

"I don't think we have any more questions, Mr. Wajir," Manning told the Zenji chief. "I hope you've told us the truth."

"I have," Wajir assured him. "You fight well. I thought all Americans were soft from easy living. I stand corrected."

"Never mind about that," Manning said in a measured tone. "Just listen to what we say. If any of your people hear anything about those murders, tell the

NSS. The longer it takes to find the terrorists, the more likely your people will be victims of vigilante groups seizing an excuse to wipe out the Islamic movement.''

"That is a good point," Wajir said with a nod.

The radio in the first Land Rover crackled to life as a voice spoke in rapid Swahili. Sergeant Ngong climbed into the vehicle and answered the call. Captain Mandera stepped closer to listen to the conversation. His scowl suggested the news was not good.

"Come on, gentlemen," the security officer told Phoenix Force. "We'd better get back to Nairobi on the double."

"What happened?" Encizo inquired.

"Somebody just tried to blow up the Soviet embassy," Mandera replied, as he strode swiftly toward the second Land Rover.

10

Columns of black smoke still streamed from the shattered windows of the Soviet embassy. Two fire trucks were parked by the sidewalk, their hoses spraying the building with water. Civilians assisted the firemen with the hoses while the police kept order among the crowds of onlookers.

Half a block from the embassy, Phoenix Force, Captain Mandera and Sergeant Ngong left the Land Rovers and struggled through the crowd till they reached the damaged building. Clustered on the lawn were several white men, most of them in civilian clothes and a few wearing the green uniforms and light blue berets of Soviet paratroopers.

"Shit," Encizo whispered softly. "This doesn't look good."

The Soviet officials were conversing angrily with Kenyan officials. The Soviet ambassador spoke at length while his translator simultaneously repeated his message in English for the Kenyan officials. Although Swahili was widely spoken throughout Kenya, all members of parliament and those engaged in business and trade spoke English. Swahili, a language derived from Arabic, Hindi, Bantu and other African tongues, lacks the extensive vocabulary needed to express the subtleties of politics and the complexities of commerce.

However, the government officials at the iron fence surrounding the embassy could not get in a word in any language as the outraged Soviets poured out demands, accusations and threats concerning the bombing of their embassy.

"Are you aware that an attack upon a Soviet embassy is an attack upon the Union of Soviet Socialist Republics itself?" the Russian translator said, speaking rapidly as he tried to keep up with the furious ambassador. "Does your government wish to declare war on the USSR? Is your country not responsible for the actions of your people? Can you not insure the protection of foreign diplomats in your country? Are you aware three Soviet citizens were killed in the explosion and five more were injured?"

"Will you please ask the ambassador to calm down for a moment?" a weary Kenyan official urged. "This bombing incident is an act of terrorism, not connected to the central government of Kenya or the KANU party...."

"Excuses will not bring our comrades back to life," the translator said when the ambassador replied to the Kenyan's remark.

As Phoenix Force stood observing the diplomats, officials and emergency personnel, McCarter felt fingers trying to ease his wallet from his hip pocket. With barely a glance at the would-be thief, he smashed his elbow into the pickpocket's breastbone and knocked him to the ground. Though startled and winded, the thief quickly got up and scrambled away. Someone in the crowd noticed what had happened and yelled, "Thief!"

Several Kenyans rapidly overtook the unlucky pickpocket. The police made no attempt to stop the vigilantes from beating the hell out of the thief, accepting the impromptu summary justice as a deterrent to crime and an outlet for citizens' frustrations.

"Hell," McCarter muttered as he watched more bystanders join the mob. "The poor bastard didn't even steal anything."

"It's the thought that counts," Calvin James remarked. "Anyway, guys, does the bombing of the embassy have any connection with the terrorism we came to investigate?"

"I doubt it," Mandera said with a frown. "The murdered people have all been Americans and West Europeans. Why would the terrorists attack the Soviet embassy?"

"Maybe they couldn't read the sign over the entrance," Encizo commented, staring at the charred remnants of an entire side of the embassy. He turned toward Manning. "What do you think of the explosion?"

"It doesn't look like anything very fancy," the Canadian demolitions expert replied. "I'd need a closer look, but my guess is somebody lobbed some grenades at the building. At least one was a thermite grenade, which is why the fire is still burning.''

"It could even have been done by somebody who figures the Russians are behind the current wave of terrorism,'' Calvin James commented. "You know, the Soviets have been hit by terrorists from time to time, too. A lot of Soviet advisors have been kidnapped or killed. They used to keep that sort of thing secret until recently, when it became public knowledge that some Russian diplomats had been kidnapped in Lebanon and the KGB had murdered the relatives of the terrorists suspected of being involved.''

"Yeah,'' Encizo recalled. "And their tactics worked. The Soviets got their people back.''

"Do you fellows resort to such ruthless techniques?'' Ngong inquired.

"No,'' McCarter assured him. "Our ruthless techniques are different. I sure wish we had some idea who to direct them at.''

"I wish we had our fifth team member with us,'' Manning said with a sigh, recalling that Yakov Katzenelenbogen spoke Russian fluently. "He'd be able to talk to the Soviets in their own language and he'd know how to set up a clandestine conference with one of the KGB officials. At least then we could get an idea whether the Soviets have any idea who bombed them.''

"Well, hell,'' McCarter growled impatiently. "I don't see any TV cameras or reporters around here.

Let's go talk to them now. That bloke speaks English."

"Wait a minute..." Encizo urged, but the headstrong Briton was already marching toward the embassy gate.

"Is he insane?" Mandera asked in astonishment.

"A borderline case," Manning replied, exasperated, as he hurried after the British ace.

McCarter shouldered his way through the crowd until he was about six feet from the gate. The Soviet ambassador and his English translator were still haranguing the frustrated Kenyan officials. A Nairobi policeman stepped in McCarter's path and held up a white-gloved palm.

"*Tafadhali,*" the cop said politely. "*Hapana...* no.*"

"*Ma-lesh,*" McCarter answered. He did not know any Swahili, but he spoke a little Arabic, acquired when he was stationed in Oman with the SAS. "It doesn't matter. This is close enough."

"Come on, damn it!" Manning snapped as he stepped behind the Briton. "This won't work...."

"Worth a try," McCarter insisted. He raised his voice as he called to the Soviet officials. "Hey, tell the ambassador we'd like to talk to him privately. Better yet, we'll just talk to you and you can chat with him afterward."

"*Shto eto, Vladimir?*" the ambassador asked his translator, as he glared at McCarter and Manning with brooding eyes beneath bushy brows.

"Never mind," Manning told them as he grabbed McCarter by the shoulder and pulled him away. "It's okay. I'm taking this guy back to the asylum."

Vladimir, the translator, whispered to the Soviet ambassador while the Canadian warrior hastily escorted McCarter away from the gate.

"When we get back to headquarters I'm going to advise Brognola to have your head examined for holes," Manning rasped as the Phoenix pair headed back toward the Land Rovers.

"Oh, hell!" McCarter replied, rolling his eyes with exasperation. "Nothing bloody happened—" Before he could finish his statement, shouts arose from the group of Russians on the embassy lawn.

"CIA!" the translator cried. "Stop them! They bombed the embassy! American war criminals!"

"Goddamn . . ." Manning hissed through clenched teeth and hurried to the vehicles.

"Well, maybe *something* happened," McCarter added, quickly following the Canadian.

Several Nairobi cops advanced, one reaching for the Smith & Wesson .38 revolver on his hip. Captain Mandera and Sergeant Ngong cut them off and flashed their ID as they tried to explain that the Russians were mistaken. However, the two Soviet paratroopers who had charged through the gate toward the Phoenix Force men ignored the NSS officers, who seemed to be protecting the "CIA bombers."

"Stop in the name of the Soviet Socialist Republic!" an Airborne junior captain exclaimed as he pulled his Makarov pistol from its leather.

The captain's attention was centered on McCarter and Manning, and he failed to notice Calvin James—a tall black man among dozens of other black men in the crowd. The Phoenix pro from the Windy City made his presence known when he launched a high side-kick to the captain's chest. The blow sent the officer staggering backward to collide with the Soviet sergeant who followed.

Rafael Encizo closed in swiftly and grabbed the AK-74 assault rifle in the Russian NCO's grasp. The Cuban warrior pulled his opponent forward and rammed a knee into the sergeant's groin. The Russian doubled up with a choking groan, and Encizo abruptly wrenched the Kalashnikov from the man's grasp.

The Soviet paratrooper raised a fist, but Encizo was quicker. He drove an uppercut to the other man's solar plexus and swiftly wrapped an arm around the Russian's neck, then smashed his other fist into his opponent's face. Stunned, the Russian just stood there until Encizo clasped his hands together and hammered them forcibly between the sergeant's shoulder blades. The Soviet NCO sprawled unconscious on the pavement.

Calvin James had stayed with the Soviet captain. The black man seized the officer's arm behind the Makarov pistol and smacked the Russian's wrist across a bent knee. The gun was jarred from the captain's grasp. Quickly, James lashed a backfist across the Russian's jaw, followed by a solid left hook. The paratrooper staggered. James pivoted with the motion of his punch to deliver a devastating sword-foot tae kwondo kick to the other man's midsection.

James growled through his teeth as he knocked the captain out cold with a hard uppercut to the jaw.

"Let's get out of here!" Gary Manning shouted, as he and McCarter ran the rest of the way to the nearest Land Rover.

The Briton slid behind the steering wheel while the Phoenix pro from Canada slithered into the back seat. James and Encizo ran to the same vehicle. Before he joined the others, however, the Cuban scooped up the unconscious Russian soldier's AK-74 rifle. McCarter started the engine just as the gates of the Soviet embassy opened wide to allow a Russian army jeep to roll into the street. Three paratroopers were in the Soviet rig—the driver and two soldiers armed with Kalashnikovs.

The crowd parted as McCarter shoved the heel of his palm into the car horn and stepped on the gas pedal. Voices roared in excitement and bewilderment. The fire and smoke from the embassy, the water spraying on the fire, the heated debates between Soviet and Kenyan officials and the presence of the NSS officers and a heavy contingent of police had already confused the bystanders.

The Land Rover carrying Phoenix Force bolted up the street and nearly collided with a minivan. On the side of the vehicle, The Voice of Kenya was painted in bold red letters. Phoenix Force had almost crashed into a television news crew on their way to cover the embassy bombing. In a hurry to reach its destination, the van pulled away from the speeding Land Rover, which was fortunate for the TV crew. Otherwise the van would surely have been hit by the Russian jeep, which sped in pursuit of the Phoenix Force vehicle.

"If McCarter comes up with any more brilliant ideas," James muttered as he opened a canvas bag to retrieve his Colt Commander .45, "I say we shoot him."

"It's not that bad!" the Briton protested, steering the Rover onto Moi Avenue.

The Soviet troops continued to follow. A soldier fired his AK from the jeep, but the motion of both vehicles spoiled his aim. A volley of 5.45 slugs tore into the road near the Phoenix Rover.

Just then a truck pulled out at the intersection with Kimathi Street. McCarter turned the wheel violently to swerve around the approaching vehicle and avoid a collision. The Soviet jeep almost succeeded as well, but its left front corner clipped the civilian vehicle. Headlights shattered. The truck skidded wildly. The Soviet rig bounced, swung back on course and sped after the Rover once more.

Sirens wailed. A Nairobi police car appeared behind the Russian jeep. McCarter continued up Moi Avenue, passing the magnificent Ismaili mosque with its great tear-shaped dome. Another cop car shot out from Jeevanjee Gardens and tried to block the path of the Phoenix Rover. Ignoring the flashing lights of the police vehicle, McCarter swung around it, the Rover scraping some shrubbery at the side of the street as it passed the police car. Passersby terrified of the speeding, swerving vehicles dashed for the safety of shops and restaurants. McCarter steered the Rover to the left and turned onto Monrovia Street, as the frustrated cop in the second police car struggled to turn his vehicle around.

Before the cop car could take off in pursuit of the Rover, the Soviet jeep arrived and tried to steer clear of the police vehicle. If the car had stayed stationary, the jeep would have missed it, but instead the jeep rear-ended the police car. Both vehicles whirled as they executed unintentional "moonshiner's spins." A Russian paratrooper screamed as he was flung from the open-topped vehicle.

Out of control, the police car crashed into a fish stand at the curb. The merchant had wisely already abandoned his post, but crates, baskets and several dozen fresh fish were scattered all over the street. The Soviet jeep connected with the unyielding metal trunk of a streetlamp.

A door of the jeep caved in, knocking the remaining rifleman into the driver. The driver was thrown forward on impact and broke his nose against the steering wheel. He cursed in Russian as he shoved his comrade aside. By then the first police car had pulled up beside the damaged Russian jeep. Two cops jumped from the vehicle and pointed Sterling MK-4 subguns at the dazed Soviets.

"Diplomatic immunity," the driver protested thickly as he raised his arms. "We want speak to someone at the Soviet embassy."

"Maybe later," a stern-faced cop replied in a harsh tone. "Get out of the car and keep your hands on your heads."

THE PHOENIX FORCE VEHICLE slowed down on University Way and turned south on Koinange Street, the direction from which they had originally come. The cops would have set up other roadblocks to the north, east and west, but the Phoenix Force hoped the police would not expect the Rover to head south again. Soon the Rover merged with traffic from the City Market area. Several other jeep-type vehicles were on the road, which helped camouflage the Phoenix rig.

"Really smooth, David," Manning complained as he disassembled the confiscated AK-74 rifle and inserted the parts in the canvas bag. "You damn near got us killed."

"I got us out of trouble, too, didn't I?" the unflappable Briton replied, with his own cockeyed brand of logic.

"Not yet," Encizo pointed out. "The police are a problem now, and even if the Soviets aren't involved in the terrorism we came to Kenya to stop, we'll still have to worry about the KGB."

"And we don't have any idea what to do next," James added grimly.

"Well, if you want my opinion—" McCarter began.

"Shut up, David," Manning cut him off. "Believe me, we've had enough of your ideas for one day."

"Just trying to help," the Briton said with a shrug, as he steered the Rover onto the avenue named after Jomo Kenyatta, the architect of Kenya's independence and the first president of Kenya.

"I think we'd better ditch this Rover," James suggested. "The cops probably have the license plates by now. Then we'll just have to lay low and contact Mandera before we make another move."

"They might decide to kick us out of the country now," Manning said glumly. "We're no closer to solving this mess than we were when we arrived four days ago. In fact, now we've probably made matters worse."

"I wouldn't say that," McCarter declared.

"No, but the rest of us would," Encizo replied, and for once McCarter didn't insist on having the last word.

"I wonder how Katz is doing?" James remarked.

"I hope he's doing better than we are," Encizo said with a weary sigh.

11

Lother Zeigler peered through the Bushnell 8 x 21 binoculars and watched the middle-aged, one-armed man with the white cane stroll along the walkway at the front of the hospital. A woman accompanied the blind man. She appeared to be in her early forties, with reddish-brown hair streaked with gray and was slightly overweight. They walked arm in arm and chatted like old friends.

The man's cane seemed thicker than those most blind men use and it had a sturdy crutch handle. Despite the white bandages covering the man's eyes, he moved with surprising confidence and dignity.

"That's him, Lother," Jurgen Tauber declared. The dark brown Ford pickup they were sitting in was parked in the hospital lot. "Colonel Yakov Katzenelenbogen. He doesn't look like much now, does he?"

"He doesn't look as sickly and helpless as you described him to me before," Zeigler said grimly. "You said he was a broken man who wouldn't get out of his hospital bed."

"I know," Tauber admitted. "He changed overnight, suddenly began to use that cane, got the prosthesis for his arm and started spending a lot of time with the woman. I think she might have encouraged him to get off his ass and start living again.''

"Who is she?'' Zeigler asked, examining her face more closely. Her features were rather plain, except for intelligent brown eyes behind horn-rimmed glasses.

"Dr. Julia Kyler,'' Tauber explained, taking a cigarillo from his pocket. "The Jew has several doctors—''

"Don't smoke that poison!'' Zeigler snapped. "Have you no respect for your body? *Der Führer* was violently opposed to tobacco. It is a filthy habit and not suitable for one of Aryan blood.''

"All right,'' Tauber agreed, tossing the cigarillo aside.

Zeigler was a fanatic about physical fitness, as his late father, General Adolf Zeigler, had also been. Lother Zeigler lifted weights three days a week, practiced karate and skied in the winter.

His devotion to ODESSA and the revival of the Nazi empire was as strong as his muscular physique. Zeigler had literally been born and bred to be a Nazi. He took great pride in the purity of his Aryan bloodlines and he believed in all the racist philosophy of the Third Reich. Most of all, Lother Zeigler believed in his father.

Lother regarded Adolf Zeigler as having been the greatest member of the National Socialist Party since Adolf Hitler and Heinrich Himmler. Greater than they were, perhaps, because they had killed themselves when the war was lost. Himmler had been taken prisoner, which Zeigler could accept as an excuse for his suicide, but he thought Hitler ought to have fled the country to continue the struggle elsewhere, just as Adolf Zeigler had.

Continuing the struggle had not been easy. Lother knew that only too well, for he had been born in the jungles of Paraguay. Of course, his mother was German, too; General Zeigler considered coupling with lesser races to be a form of bestiality and never strayed from the principles of ethnic purity and racial supremacy.

That such a great man should have been persecuted by Jewish filth was outrageous, in Lother Zeigler's opinion. The Israelis had attacked an ODESSA base in Southern France, and the one-armed racial inferior who now walked arm in arm with the female doctor had almost killed General Zeigler.

Lother still recalled his horror when his father returned from Europe. His face had been slashed from eyebrow to cheek, his eye sliced in half like an olive. The Israeli colonel had clawed him with his steel hook and had then driven a bayonet into the general's abdomen. A lesser man would have died, but not Adolf Zeigler. Lother considered his father to be Christlike in his virtue and devotion, sacrifice and courage. But godlike men are damned to suffer in an imperfect world, and even the sons of Odin eventually faced their twilight.

General Zeigler recovered from the wounds he had suffered in France and eventually supervised another European operation for ODESSA. It had been a bold plan to reclaim Germany for the shadow empire of the SS brotherhood and unite East and West Germany to form a mighty power that would dominate Europe, if not the entire world.

The plan had failed and the same one-armed Jew, identified as Katzenelenbogen, had been reported in Austria by General Zeigler himself. Finally, another terrorist scheme involving assassinations in France was foiled, and General Adolf Zeigler had to choose between taking his own life or surrendering. Naturally he chose the honorable solution—just as Himmler had done. Perhaps, Lother Zeigler had thought after hearing news of his beloved father's death, *der Führer* had chosen the right path as well. He was certain his father could not have lived with a third failure on his soul. How much worse was the agony suffered by Adolf Hitler on seeing the fall of his entire Reich? How could any man, even a god-man, continue after such a dreadful blow?

Lother Zeigler had long dreamed of the day he would find and destroy the one-armed Jew. Yakov Katzenelenbogen had become the personification of evil in the twisted mind of the young Nazi fanatic. He personally blamed the Israeli for the failures of ODESSA and for the death of his father. Lother craved revenge with a burning passion as fierce as his love for his father. He had sworn vengeance, and now the opportunity had arrived.

Zeigler had fantasized many times about torturing the Jew, but he realized now that might not be practical. Torture required time, and there would be little of that. Zeigler had noticed the two men dressed in neat gray suits and striped ties who tagged along behind Katz and Julia Kyler. They were government agents of some sort. If Zeigler kidnapped Katzenelenbogen, he would need to take him somewhere and spend at least a day there to make torture worthwhile, which would be risky with feds on the trail.

Nein, Zeigler thought in the language of his father. He would have to be content with killing the Jew, but he would make certain Katz knew who his executioner was and why he was about to die. And his death would not be quick and painless.

"I have a rifle buried at a site outside of town," Tauber told Zeigler. "A black-market gun dealer from Washington, D.C. sold it to me a while back. A .30-06 bolt-action Springfield. With a scope and silencer, we could turn the weapon into a good sniper rifle. Then, when the old Jew takes a walk around the lawn—"

"No," Zeigler replied. "I want to see his face when I tell him why he's going to die. I want him to know what's happening."

"What about the bodyguards?" Tauber asked. "There are always two men protecting him, government agents."

"FBI?" Zeigler inquired as he lowered the binoculars.

"Department of Justice," Tauber answered. "Killing him inside the hospital could be complicated."

"You're an orderly there," Zeigler stated. "You shouldn't have any trouble getting me a uniform. We should be able to forge an ID card if necessary."

"You plan to impersonate an orderly?" Tauber frowned. "That may be unwise. Everybody in the hospital knows everybody else."

"I doubt that they'll find a new orderly suspicious," Zeigler answered. "But we'll have to plan this carefully, because one chance is all we'll get. If we fail, they'll move the Jew to another place."

"When do we strike?" Tauber asked.

"When we're certain the time is right," Zeigler replied with a wiry smile. "Soon, my friend. We'll just have to be patient for a day or two longer."

HAL BROGNOLA ENTERED the gymnasium. It was a small room, available to a very restricted list of personnel. At the center of the floor the Fed noticed a judo mat, whose dents suggested it had been used recently. Special Agent Renko was dressed in shorts and T-shirt, working out on a weight bench. The other Justice man assigned to protect Katzenelenbogen, Special Agent Farley, stood across the room with a bamboo sword in his fists.

Yakov Katzenelenbogen, clad in a baggy gray sweat suit, was busy working out on a heavy bag suspended from the ceiling. Wielding his cane with his left hand, the Israeli pounded the bag, throwing in an occasional punch with the steel hooks of his prosthesis.

"I'll be damned," Brognola whispered as he watched Katz deftly strike and jab with the cane, then dodge the heavy bag when it swung back from a hard blow.

Again Katz parried the bag with the cane, then hooked a kick into it. The bag swung around in a wide arc toward the blind man. His left arm punched the bag with the crutch handle of his cane and then slashed the shaft across the target.

Brognola was about to approach Katz when he was startled by a shrill cry.

"Haaii-yaa!" Agent Farley shouted the classic *kiai* as he attacked Katz with the bamboo sword.

Katz whirled to meet the attack, raising the cane to block the sword overhead. Farley tried to swing the bamboo weapon in a roundhouse stroke, but Katz's cane seemed to cling to the sword and followed the movement. The Israeli jerked his right arm in a short punch, careful not to strike out in earnest for fear of hitting Farley with the steel hooks of his prosthesis.

Farley thrust with the sword. Katz parried the stroke, then sidestepped and suddenly shoved the shaft of his cane into the agent's chest. Farley lost his balance and fell to the mat. Katz raised his cane and simulated a downward stroke.

Brognola almost raised a cheer, but then noticed Agent Renko had left the weights by the bench and was approaching. "Hello sir," he said. "I didn't expect you...."

"Obviously," the Fed said dryly. "It's lucky it was I who came in here and not an enemy assassin. You guys are suppose to protect Katz, not pump iron."

"He wanted to work out," Renko explained. "For an older guy, he's in damn good shape. You wouldn't guess it, 'cause he's got sort of a potbelly, but that's one tough dude."

"I know," Brognola said with a nod. "If his eyes weren't bandaged, I wouldn't believe he was blind. He handles that cane pretty good."

"He's unbelievable, sir," Renko agreed. "The past couple of days we've been practicing judo with him. He takes off the artificial arm to avoid hurting us with those steel hooks. Have you ever had the stuffing bounced out of you by a one-armed blind man? I would have felt humiliated if you hadn't told me this guy was some kind of superprofessional."

"He's adjusted to blindness that well in less than a week?" Brognola raised his eyebrows with astonishment.

"Yakov isn't an ordinary man," Renko confirmed. "I think Dr. Kyler has helped him a lot, too, but even that's not enough to explain how Yakov has come so far so soon. Guess he's had experience dealing with a handicap before."

"You're right," Brognola said. "Katz is no ordinary man."

"Mr. Brown?" Katz approached, referring to Brognola by his most recent cover name. "Is that you?"

"Recognize my voice from across the room?" The Fed walked toward Katz. "I didn't think we were talking that loud."

"I'm learning to rely on my listening ability," Katz replied as he walked toward Brognola. "It's nice to talk to you again."

"And we need to talk privately." Brognola turned to the two Justice agents. "Mind waiting outside?"

"Of course not, sir," Renko agreed. He and Farley left the gym.

Wood tapped wood as Katz used his cane to feel for the bench. He sat down and placed the cane across his knees, and Brognola joined him.

"When do the bandages come off?" the Fed asked.

"Three days," Katz replied. "I'm hoping I'll be able to see, but I'm trying to prepare for the worst if it turns out otherwise."

"Pretty impressive," the Fed stated. "Renko and Farley seem humbled by your ability."

"Ability or not, a blind man can't work in the field, Hal," Katz stated. "I realize that. Judo and stick fighting aren't the same as taking on terrorists with submachine guns. I can probably still hold my own against muggers, but I won't be able to go into combat again if I'm still blind after the bandages come off."

"Any idea of what you'll want to do if..." Brognola let the sentence trail off.

"I've started to learn braille," Katz answered. "Maybe I could take up writing as a full-time job. I wrote a couple of books on archaeology, you know. I can also work as a translator or a teacher for some government agency. I don't want to be stuck at a desk, but I have to face facts. In a few more years you'd have to retire me from Phoenix Force, anyway."

"Not for a while," Brognola assured him. "Not as long as you can do your job as well as you have in the past. Frankly, I don't think I could find a man to replace you. And I know the others feel the same way."

"Any idea how their mission in Kenya is going?" Katz asked. "Don't violate security if you don't think I should know any details. I'll understand."

"I'm not worried about you," the Fed assured him. "I don't think it's gone too well so far. Did you hear about the Soviet embassy being bombed?"

"It was on the radio," Katz replied. "I wondered if the Force was involved."

"No," Brognola answered, "but they were chased all over Nairobi by the police and a jeep full of Soviet guardsmen."

"I wonder what McCarter did to cause that," the Israeli said with a sigh. "Well, I assume they avoided capture?"

"So far," the Fed answered. "But the problem is that nobody is sure if the bombing of the embassy is connected with the terrorism Phoenix Force was sent to deal with. I can tell you this much—that a series of murders of Western Europeans and Americans was the reason for the mission.''

"Terrorists killing individuals from Western democracies, right?'' Katz mused thoughtfully. "And now the Soviets have been hit. Unless the political situation in Kenya is much more volatile than I thought, the two incidents must be connected.''

"It could be a group of radicals striking out at the Soviets because they figure the commies are responsible for the murders,'' Brognola suggested.

"That's possible,'' Katz replied, "but not very likely. If the victims were Kenyans, it might make more sense.''

"Maybe it's some sort of Islamic Holy War terrorism,'' the Fed wondered out loud. "Kenya doesn't have a Muslim majority, but there's a large Islamic population there that's been taking a lot of heat over the terrorism. Some people think they're responsible because the terrorists claim to be connected to Idi Amin.''

"Amin?'' Katz smiled. "I can't image him trying to move into Kenya. That's like Hitler trying to take over Israel. This terrorism sounds like classic Marighella philosophy.''

"Marighella?'' Brognola asked. "Didn't he write the *Mini Manual of Terrorism*?''

"Right,'' Katz confirmed. "The theory is to cause so much unrest in a nation that the host government overreacts to the threat. When the country becomes an internal dictatorship, then it's easier to rally support for an all-out revolution. Marighella was a Marxist, and most terrorists who use his concepts are also. The KGB is usually pulling the strings of such groups. I heard on the news that the assistant ambassador at the Soviet embassy was killed in the bombing.''

''You think the KGB would be ruthless enough to set off the bomb in their own embassy in order to throw our people off the track.''

''I wouldn't put much past the KGB,'' Katz answered, ''but it does seem unlikely. The price is pretty high for a scheme that could easily fail. Kenya is pro-Western. That means they wouldn't be swayed to accept Communism easily. At least, not Soviet-backed Communism.''

''What do you mean?'' Brognola asked.

''It could be some splinter group of Marxists who endorse Third World unity under socialism,'' Katz remarked. ''Whoever they are, they must have been in Kenya for a long time to put together the organization necessary for something like this. I suggest you have Aaron check on possible suspects. Former dictators in exile, like Idi Amin, but more likely ones who had good relations with Kenya before they got bounced out of office could be responsible. Maybe some outfit that used to be a powerful political force in Africa but has been forced underground for some reason.''

''I'll have the Bear check into it,'' Brognola assured him. ''Yakov, I want you to know, however things turn out, you'll always be part of Stony Man operations.''

"Thank you," Katz said with a nod. "We'll just have to see what happens. Speaking of which, I'd better finish my workout so I can get back to the hospital. Dr. Kyler promised to bring me a tape recorder and some Tchaikovsky cassettes.''

"Okay." Brognola placed a hand on Katz's shoulder. "I'll be in touch, Yakov."

12

"The president of my country has had a long conversation with the President of the United States," Captain Mandera said to the assembled members of Phoenix Force, as he paced the floor of his office at National Security Service headquarters in Nairobi. "They discussed your mission and whether to allow you to continue, since matters have hardly improved since your arrival."

"So what's the verdict?" Rafael Encizo asked. The Cuban sat on the edge of Mandera's desk, leafing through a copy of the *Daily Nation*, Kenya's leading English-language newspaper.

"You can stay for another week," Mandera replied, his tone suggesting he was not certain he wanted them to remain in Kenya that long. "If you haven't made any progress by that time, you'll have to leave or be placed under arrest and expelled from the country."

"I guess everybody's getting impatient," Gary Manning remarked, pouring himself a cup of coffee. "Can't say I blame them."

"We've done our best," David McCarter said with a shrug.

"And so far our best has sucked, man," Calvin James muttered glumly. He was examining a map of Kenya with tiny flags pinned to the areas where terrorist incidents had occurred. "We've been barking up the wrong trees so far. Gotta find the right one real soon."

"Hello, gents," Sergeant Ngong announced as he entered the office with a thick pile of teletype sheets in his hand. "Glad I found you all here together."

"You'd better have an excuse for sounding so damn cheerful," Encizo said, glancing at the papers in Ngong's hand. "Did you bring us good news?"

"Maybe," the sergeant answered as he placed the sheets on the desk. "This material arrived via communications satellite. It was in code, and we had to translate it. Apparently, somebody back in the States has some theories about who the terrorists may be."

"Let's take a look," Manning said as he unfolded the material.

The data had been assembled by Aaron Kurtzman, the Stony Man computer wizard, based on Yakov Katzenelenbogen's suggestions to Brognola. The sheets of paper listed leaders of various political groups in Africa, some active and some inactive.

At the head of the list was Milton Obote, who had been president of Uganda before Idi Amin and who later took office after Amin was forced into exile, then was himself thrown out of office again. Obote had not been much of an improvement over Amin. "Big Daddy" Idi was believed responsible for killing about three hundred thousand Ugandans during his time in office. Obote was suspected of killing close to one hundred thousand of his countrymen. When General Tito Okello led a military coup in July of 1985, Obote fled the country—to Kenya.

"Any idea what Obote's been up to since he wound up in your country?" Manning asked Mandera.

"I'll find out," the security officer promised.

Other possible suspects were remnants of the old Masie regime of Equatorial Guinea. Masie, whose real name was Francisco Macias Nguema, was a brutal dictator who tortured and murdered approximately forty thousand of his countrymen before he was overthrown and tried and executed for genocide. Some members of his vicious regime had managed to flee the country, and their whereabouts were unknown.

Also listed among the suspects were remnants of Derge, the 120-man Ethiopian military committee that came to power after Haile Selassie was deposed. The Derge military junta ended when General Teferi Bante and ten of his followers were killed in a shootout. Lt. Colonel Mengistu Halie Mariam took power, and Ethiopia soon became a Communist state. The fate of Derge remained a mystery for news out of Ethiopia was sketchy and unreliable. The remaining members might have been executed, or might even have changed sides to join the Marxist government. Or they might have slipped across the border into Kenya.

Perhaps the strangest suggestion among the data Phoenix Force were now studying was that a remnant of Chinese military advisors could be involved. Under Mao's leadership in the 1960s, thousands of Chinese military and intelligence personnel were active throughout Africa, especially in the Congo region. Originally they had worked with Soviet advisors, until the Russian Bear and the Chinese Dragon had a falling-out. Eventually, the Soviets pretty well muscled the Chinese out of African politics. Since Mao's death, China had concentrated on domestic concerns instead of foreign revolutions, but there could still be some diehards among the Maoists that remained in Africa.

"Do you figure this theory about the Chinese was thrown in as a joke?" Calvin James inquired after reading the list.

"I doubt it," Manning replied. He turned to Captain Mandera. "What do you think?"

"There's a very small number of Asians living in Kenya," the security officer answered. "They're not terribly popular. President Kenyatta expelled thousands of Asian businessmen and shopkeepers during the late sixties and early seventies. I don't think any of the Orientals who remain have ever been regarded as potential terrorists or political threats."

"Let's check into the possibility anyway," Manning urged. "Many things in this strange world don't make any sense. If a Hollywood movie star can become President of the United States, anything is possible."

LATER THAT DAY, Phoenix Force paid another visit to Captain Mandera after he had had security and immigration files checked. With the aid of computers, technicians had searched the immigration files on Asians living in Kenya, starting with Chinese who had emigrated from other countries in Africa since 1960. Most of these earned modest incomes from small businesses in the cities. However, a pair of recent immigrants caught the attention of Phoenix Force. Chou Ziyang and Li Yuann had brought to Kenya with them a nest egg of hundreds of thousands of CFA francs, a form of currency used by several Central African countries. One CFA franc was worth roughly one-fifth of a cent in American currency. Chou and Li had purchased some land near Mount Nyiru, and within five years had established a successful tea plantation. They were making a comfortable profit by selling what their advertisements called "Chinese-African tea, grown in Kenya and processed with eight thousand years of Oriental experience." Their tea was one of the most expensive brands available in Kenya, and sold well to European markets.

Chou and Li were known to employ a large number of young Kenyans, and they had connections with traders in other African nations. The two Chinese had also received authorization from the Central Firearms Bureau to keep automatic weapons at the plantation for protection. They owned at least two trucks, two cars and a helicopter.

"I think we ought to check these blokes out," McCarter declared, examining the computer printout on Chou and Li.

"Oh, no!" Manning groaned. "Something's wrong. If he's got the same idea I have, I'm worried."

"Piss off," the Briton growled.

"Let's try to do this right this time," James urged. "I mean, since we arrived in Kenya we've either gone down blind alleys or just plain fucked up."

"I've got an idea how we can visit the plantation without making the Chinese suspicious," Encizo announced. "Well, they might be sort of suspicious, but the plan won't upset them if they're innocent and it shouldn't scare them into bolting if they're guilty."

"Does it include any provisions for them to decide to shoot us on sight?" James inquired.

"If that happens, we're dead," Encizo replied with a grin. "But if they give us a chance to communicate, I think we'll be okay."

"Is communicating going to be a problem?" Manning double-checked the file. "I don't see anything here concerning languages spoken. Maybe they only speak Chinese and some Swahili."

"They speak English," Mandera assured the Canadian. "Anyone in Kenya who runs a business like theirs speaks English."

"The tea plantation is located in the Rift Valley region," Sergeant Ngong remarked. "That's quite a distance away, and difficult terrain to cover by Land Rover."

"They have a helipad for their chopper," Encizo stated. "Can you get us a helicopter?"

"Probably," Mandera said with a sigh. "But we'll have trouble finding a pilot we can trust to keep security intact."

"No, you won't," McCarter said cheerfully. "You're looking at the best possible pilot for the mission."

"You can fly a helicopter?" Ngong asked.

"I can fly anything, mate," McCarter assured him.

"Yeah," Encizo said dryly. "You just have a little trouble landing sometimes."

"What the hell are you talking about?" the Briton demanded. "That glider in the Bahamas? I had to land it on a helicopter pad with two choppers in the way."

"I was thinking of the Beechcraft in California," Encizo replied. "You broke the wings off it."

"I landed it on a bloody gravel driveway, and I didn't break the wings until the plane hit the gate that was in the way," McCarter insisted.

"Oh, God," Mandera groaned as he pressed his hand to his forehead. "One way or another, I'll be glad when you fellows go home."

THE AMERICAN-MADE SEAHAWK hovered over the Rift Valley. Forests of copal, baobab and teak reached up to the sky. Monkeys scrambled about in the branches and leaped from tree to tree, chattering in alarm. On open ground small antelopes bounded away, frightened by the roar of the helicopter's whirling rotors.

"That's it!" James had to shout to be heard above the thunder of the chopper engine. "There's the plantation up ahead."

Below was a one-hundred-acre expanse of land covered with tea plants, which varied in height from four to ten feet and resembled small willow trees with long leather leaves. McCarter grunted as he glanced down at the fields.

"Something wrong?" asked James, who was seated beside McCarter.

"Yeah," the Briton answered. "Something's wrong with this plantation. It's going to hell. Look at the size of those tea plants."

"Christ," James muttered, gazing down at the crop below. "I thought they were trees. You sure those are tea plants?"

"Positive," McCarter assured him. "I saw lots of tea plantations in Formosa. Tea plants will grow pretty tall, more than thirty feet in the wild. But any plantation worth a damn prunes the plants constantly to keep them about two or three feet high. This crop has been neglected for some time."

"That's interesting," Manning commented from a back seat. "Chou and Li didn't build a successful tea business by goofing off. Maybe they've been busy doing something else."

"Let's not jump to conclusions," Encizo urged. "Maybe they're just short of workers, or they've branched into a different business and let the tea crop slip."

"There's nothing in their files to suggest another source of income," Manning reminded him. "But you're right, Rafael. Neglected crops don't prove the Chinese are terrorists."

The copter approached the heart of the plantation. The main house was a long one-story structure of adobe brick. Several smaller wood shacks formed a semicircle facing the main house like a giant C. The helipad was simply a large clearing in the center. Two choppers were already parked on the ground below.

"Attention, pilot of the helicopter!" a voice announced in crisp English through the radio of the Seahawk. "This is private property, not an airstrip. You are not authorized to land here. Please, move on."

McCarter gathered up the microphone and pressed the transmit button. "This is Jonathan McCall, international pilot's license B72758535," he announced. "Request permission to land for inspection of my aircraft which may be in need of repairs."

"Permission denied," the voice replied. "There is an airfield eighty kilometers southeast of here, near the South Turkana National Park. I'm certain they will assist you."

"I hear something rattling about in my bloody engine," McCarter said sharply. "I'm not going to try to fly eighty bleedin' kilometers, my engine might quit before I reach the damn airfield. Sorry about the invasion of privacy, but I'm landing this bird and I'm doing it right now."

"Trespassing is a serious offense here," the voice warned. "We are within our rights if we shoot trespassers. Shoot to kill. Do you understand me, sir?"

"You want to shoot us, that's up to you, mate," McCarter spoke into the microphone. "But the central government knows we're in this area and they're aware we planned to stop at your plantation anyway, even before the engine trouble occurred. You folks want to have trouble with the government, then you can kill us. Personally, I'd rather be shot than burn to death in a chopper crash, anyway."

"Permission to land confirmed." There was a trace of anger in the voice.

"Thank you for your cooperation," McCarter stated. "Over and out."

"Nobody wants us to visit them," James remarked. "The Zenji didn't want us. The Soviet ambassador sicced his guards on us. Even Captain Mandera said he'd be glad when we went home. Maybe we should try a different mouthwash."

McCarter did not join in the conversation, although wiseass remarks usually appealed to him. The

Briton was busy with the helicopter controls. Below, several figures approached the helipad, most of them carrying firearms.

"This plan doesn't seem as good as it did when we talked about it earlier," Calvin James remarked as he watched the armed men circle the helipad.

"Just follow the script," Encizo urged. "Everything will be okay... I hope"

McCarter eased the cyclic controls and worked the rudders to descend slowly. The Seahawk landed smoothly. Manning slid open a cabin door and emerged from the aircraft with a video camera braced on his shoulder. Encizo followed, a cassette tape recorder slung across his shoulder and a 35 mm camera hanging around his neck.

"Hello." The Cuban greeted the men on the ground with a nervous smile. "We're with Docu-Drama International Foundation of Independent Film Makers, Limited. Here's my card...."

"Sifamahu." A black African with a Sterling submachine gun in his fists looked puzzled.

"Jambo sana," Calvin James greeted, speaking about one-fourth of all the Swahili he recalled from an African Studies course in college. *"Habari?"*

"Hapana mzuri," a grim-faced African replied as he snapped back the bolt of his French MAT-49 machine pistol.

"The conversation doesn't sound so good," Manning commented.

"It doesn't sound any better in Swahili," James replied.

"You told us you had engine trouble," a wiry Chinese announced as he approached the visitors. "You did not say anything about being part of some movie crew."

Phoenix Force recognized Chou Ziyang from a photograph in the NSS files. But although the records had described the man's approximate height and build, they had failed to mention his rigid posture or the catlike grace of his movement. The photo in the security files had not captured the fierce intensity of Chou's dark eyes.

Chou wore light blue cotton trousers and a blue jacket with a high mandarin collar and frog buttons. On his head perched a conical hat of woven rice reeds. A gunbelt was buckled around his narrow waist with a pistol in a button-flap holster on his hip.

"We're having engine problems," McCarter assured him as he waited for the rotor blades gradually to stop spinning. "I have to climb up on top of her to check the turbines."

"I am familiar with the construction of helicopters," Chou replied in a flat voice.

"You a pilot too, mate?" the Briton inquired.

"Yes, I am," the Chinese replied, but he turned toward the other three Phoenix Force members. "What is this rubbish about filming a documentary? This is private property, and we do not wish to be disturbed in this manner."

"Hold on, mister," Encizo began. "True, we weren't really up front with you when we were in the air, but we didn't lie, either. We really do have engine trouble, we really needed to land and the Central Government really does know we're here."

"This is not government property," Chou insisted.

"We realize that, sir," Manning stated, holding the video camera by its carrying handle at his side. "We don't want to invade your privacy, but you might change your mind about this if you hear what we're trying to do here."

"Perhaps we should listen to them," Li Yuann said urgently as he stepped forward. "What can it hurt? We have no terrible dark secrets to hide. This is a tea plantation, not an opium center."

Li was slightly shorter than his partner, but was dressed in a similar Mao jacket and coolie hat. A bit overweight, with a moon-shaped face, Li seemed less threatening than his steely-eyed comrade. But Phoenix Force had learned long ago that appearances can be deceiving and that underestimating an opponent can be a fatal mistake.

"What we're trying to do is simple," James began. "We're trying to film the Africa most people never see. Most Americans and Europeans still think of Africa as mostly jungle with half-naked black savages running around. Oh, they might know about the whites and the blacks fighting each other in South Africa, and some of them might remember Uganda, but that's only because of Idi Amin. They might even remember the Congo, but that's usually because they recall the mercenary wars of the sixties.''

"Congo?" one of the African gunmen said with alarm in his voice.

Chou turned sharply and held up a hand to silence the man. Meanwhile McCarter had climbed onto the Seahawk and had lifted the bonnet to check the turbines. The Briton hummed as he took a wrench from a tool kit and reached inside the engine.

"Westerners also know about Ethiopia, thanks to the 'We are the World' song and video and the Live Aid and Band Aid efforts to raise money to feed starving people there," Manning added. "But when people think of Kenya they usually think of the national parks and the animals there, not the people. We want to show the people of Africa, especially the people that the rest of the world doesn't think of as Africans.''

"People like you," Encizo continued in the same vein. "Two Chinese who fled the Communist mainland to become successful capitalists in Africa. A great story."

"We're not interested in your cheap sensationalist journalism and simpleminded propaganda," Chou said angrily.

"My partner means that we don't wish the publicity," Li Yuann explained. "You see, we try to keep a low profile."

"You sell tea on the international market," Manning stated. "That's not exactly a state secret, Mr. Chou."

"I'm Li," the Asian said. "He's Chou."

"Sorry," Manning replied. Of course, he knew the identity of each man from the NSS photos in Nairobi. The Canadian pro had called Li "Chou" on purpose to imply that he knew very little about the two Chinese.

"Gentlemen," Li began. "You must understand that Asians are not well-liked here in Kenya. Our tea may be popular with Europeans, but prudence requires that in Kenya we publicize only our product, not ourselves personally. A strange irony."

David McCarter had quietly climbed down from the Seahawk and had strolled to the two helicopters belonging to the plantation owners. One of the craft was an American-made Bell UH-1, a large military chopper capable of carrying fourteen men. The UH-1 had been used successfully in Vietnam, and some of the surplus gunships had been sold to foreign nations friendly to the U.S., including Kenya. In 1982 the KANU government had disbanded their 2,100-man air force because many of its members had supported the rebellion against the central government. Apparently some of the military aircraft had wound up on the civilian market.

The other helicopter intrigued McCarter. It was older than the Bell, constructed of heavier metal alloys. Its current coat of dark gray paint was recent, and chips here and there revealed that it had formerly been brown and, before that, green. McCarter knelt by the tail pylon and smiled thinly when he saw the manufacturer number, the abbreviation CCCP and two words in Cyrillic letters.

"Looking for something?" Chou Ziyang demanded, glaring at McCarter.

"Just taking a look at your choppers," the Briton said, patting the battered old copter. "This one's new to me. Never flew one of these. It's a German Flederfuchs, isn't it?"

"Yes," Chou said, smiling. "You certainly know your aircraft, Mr.... McCall, isn't it?"

"That's right," the British ace said with a nod. "You know, I generally fly out of Nairobi. I don't recall seeing you or your choppers at the airport."

"I don't get out there very often," Chou answered. "You're British, aren't you? Been in Kenya long?"

"Not really," McCarter said with a shrug.

"I've always wanted to fly a British Whirlwind HAR-10," Chou said wistfully. "I understand it is a wonderful craft."

"It is," McCarter confirmed. "Uses a Rolls-Royce Gnome turboshaft engine. Purrs like a kitten, a lovely copter."

"Perhaps I'll still get the chance," the Chinese remarked. "Do you need a hand with your repairs?"

"All taken care of," McCarter assured him. "I'm just waiting for you to throw these movie-making snoops off your property. I suppose they'll want to go take pictures of the bleeding Masai tribesmen next. But as long as I get paid for flying them around, it makes no difference to me."

"You have my sympathies." Chou laughed. "If you ever get your hands on another Whirlwind HAR-10, fly her over here. I'll pay you to let me take her up for an hour or two."

13

"Those guys are hiding something," James remarked as the Seahawk rose from the plantation with Phoenix Force aboard. "Did you notice how one of the gunmen reacted when I mentioned the Congo?"

"He's probably from the Congo," Manning commented. "He had a MAT-49 subgun. Those French nine-millimeter blasters have been floating around the Congo for two decades."

"I remember seeing MAT-49s in Nam too," James recalled. "The NVA liked to convert the old French guns to 7.62 mm so they'd use the same ammo as Kalashnikovs."

"That extra helicopter they've got is probably from the Congo or one of the other Marxist African countries, too," McCarter stated as he flew the Seahawk across the fields of neglected tea plants. "I asked Chou if it was a German Flederfuchs and he said it was, but it isn't a German chopper."

"You're sure?" Manning asked.

"I found a factory number under the tail," the Briton answered. "And the initials CCCP."

"What's that supposed to mean?" James asked with a frown.

"Union of Soviet Socialist Republics," Rafael Encizo explained.

"There was more Russian printed on the chopper, but I have no idea what it meant," McCarter continued. "Probably the name of the factory where the helicopter was built."

"So Chou and Li have spent time in the Congo and obviously have some connections with the military there," Manning mused. "The Red Chinese used to have a lot of influence in that portion of Africa."

"I don't think either one of them is older than thirty-five," James commented. "They're too young to be veterans of the conflicts in the Congo during the sixties."

"Apparently they moved to Africa shortly after Mao Tse-tung died," Encizo remarked. "The Chinese government has seemed pretty friendly to the West lately, but it's still Communist, and that means it has a political philosophy contrary to ours. It's possible Chou and Li are enemy agents working for Peking."

"They don't fit the profile for SAD agents," McCarter stated. "Intelligence agents from the Chinese Social Affairs Department would keep a very low profile here in Kenya. They might have an advisor running an operation from the Chinese embassy, but they wouldn't have field agents handling it directly. Cut-out operators would handle that. Local Africans, not Chinese."

"I don't think it's government-sponsored terror-ism, either," Manning added. "But we can't even prove Chou and Li are involved."

"Do you think they're legitimate businessmen?" Encizo asked.

"No," Manning answered. "I've got a gut feeling that we've found the enemy headquarters, but we won't get the Kenyan government to agree to a raid. Not with what we've got so far."

"But we might get more evidence," McCarter said cheerfully. "I planted a limpet microphone on the undercarriage of their commie chopper. It transmits a radio wave to the receiver built into our Seahawk. At this very moment, any conversation by the Chinese and their African allies is being tape-recorded."

McCarter opened a compartment hatch near his seat to reveal the radio receiver, with a connecting cable linked to a cassette tape recorder. The spools of the recorder turned as the radio fed data directly into it.

"Nice work, David," Manning declared. "Maybe there's hope for you yet. I just hope they didn't find the microphone."

"We'll know they did if we hear Mary Had a Little Lamb in mandarin Chinese," James commented. "How far is the range on that radio microphone?"

"Only about two miles," McCarter answered. He gazed out at the twilight sky. "We can fly around the plantation for a few minutes before we head for the airstrip at Lake Turkana. We need to refuel before we try to return to Nairobi. I sure don't want to attempt a forced landing after dark because we ran out of petrol.''

"I'll be glad to get our hands on our weapons again,'' James confessed. "Going into enemy territory without a gun makes me more nervous than being guest of honor at a KKK convention.''

"Yeah,'' Manning agreed. "But we couldn't carry any guns when we paid Chou and Li a visit. We were supposed to be newsmen, not mercenaries. We couldn't even risk carrying a gun in the chopper, since tourists can't bring firearms into the country without special permission from the government. It's part of the ban on hunting here.''

"Seems to me I've seen a lot of people packing guns since we arrived,'' James muttered. "Maybe we've just been hanging around with the wrong crowd.''

"Hanging around with the wrong crowd is part of our job,'' Encizo said with a shrug.

NIGHT HAD FALLEN when the Seahawk approached the Turkana airfield. McCarter scanned the field with a searchlight, noting two unlighted runways. The only aircraft to be seen was a twin-engine Mooney near a hangar. There were no lights on in the headquarters building.

"Something's wrong,'' McCarter announced tensely. "There's no response to my radio call for permission to land.''

"The place looks deserted," James remarked, glancing out the window. "Are you sure it's still operational?"

"There's a plane down there," the Briton answered. "We need fuel, so we're going to have to land anyway."

"If the airfield is deserted and has no fuel," Encizo commented, "you'll be burning up a lot of gas by landing and taking off again."

"It's a chance we've got to take," McCarter insisted. "We'll never reach Nairobi with what we've got. Even if there's no one around, we might find enough fuel to get us back to home base."

The Seahawk descended to a clearing near the office building, which was really a one-story house, so small it could have only one or two rooms. McCarter landed the chopper and shut down the engine, and Phoenix Force emerged from the Seahawk and headed for the office, heads bowed in a reflex action to avoid the blades of the rotor still spinning above them.

The office windows were dark, like the empty eye sockets of a skull. Nothing moved except some loose sheets of newspaper blown across the ground by the air currents caused by the helicopter blades. Instinctively, the four combat veterans sensed something sinister about the unnatural stillness.

Suddenly the office door opened. A large African in a black turtleneck stepped onto the porch and smiled at them. His hands were hidden behind his back. Phoenix Force had not seen the muscular black before.

"Good evening, gentlemen," the African declared as he brought his arms forward and revealed the Walther P-38 pistol in his fist. "We're glad you could make it."

Six men filed out the door behind him, bizarre figures, dressed in leopard-skin capes. The cat heads had been fashioned into crude masks and were perched on top of the men's skulls. The forelegs of the leopard skins were strapped to the men's arms; their hands were covered by spotted fur mittens from which four steel claws extended. Beneath the capes, some of the men wore loincloths; others were clad in khaki trousers or walking shorts. All wore leopard-skin footgear that resembled moccasins, complete with claws.

"After all," the African in charge of the leopardmen continued, "this is *your* funeral."

He gestured with the German pistol and the six killers in leopard costume uttered wild war cries and charged toward the four unarmed members of Phoenix Force.

The scene was an encounter from a nightmare, recalling the primitive times when wild creatures with fangs and claws preyed on human flesh.

Phoenix Force had confronted a great variety of dangerous opponents in the past, but on this occasion none of them carried firearms for support. Less experienced men might have been petrified with fear, but the four Phoenix pros stood their ground and met their beast-like opponents head-on.

As the first leopard-man closed in and attacked Gary Manning, the Canadian warrior ducked to avoid a claw swipe. He clasped his hands together and swung a pile-driver blow under the African assassin's ribs, propelling him into the path of another killer in a spotted cape.

Both leopard-men staggered off balance. Before they could recover from the surprise, Manning quickly attacked the first man from behind, hammering a fist between his opponent's shoulder blades. Then Manning grabbed the stunned African and rammed the guy's forehead into the face of the second leopard-man. Gripping the first opponent's cat cape in one fist, he thrust his other hand between the killer's legs, grabbed and pulled hard. The African shrieked as Manning picked him up and used him as a battering ram to knock the other leopard-man to the ground.

Manning dumped the first opponent on top of the second and kicked the unlucky African in the side of the head until he was unconscious. The second leopard-man slashed his claw-hand at the Canadian's leg, and sharp pain lanced Manning's calf as a steel talon tore cloth and skin.

Manning jumped back, and the African tried to rise. The Phoenix pro shoved a boot into the unconscious leopard-man and pushed him across the chest of the assassin who was about to get to his feet. The African grunted as he landed flat on his back. Manning dropped on top of the unconscious hit man to pin the other clawed opponent to the ground and hammered his big fist into the man's face three times till he was sure he was out cold.

David McCarter had stooped and grabbed a fistful of dirt as a leopard-man charged toward him. Before the leopard-man could swing a clawed fist, the British ace hurled the dirt into the unprotected eyes of his opponent.

The African snarled and cursed and struck out blindly. McCarter dodged the wild claw stroke and stamped a side-kick to the African's kneecap, crushing the cartilage in the joint. The leopard-man cried out. He tried to swing a backhand stroke at the Briton, but McCarter caught his opponent's arm at the wrist and elbow. He twisted with one hand and pushed with the other to apply a straight-arm bar and forced his opponent to the ground.

The African's face hit the dirt. McCarter pinned the guy's arm under a knee to hold him down. The Briton's hand chopped twice across the base of the African's neck. The leopard-man stopped struggling.

Two leopard-men attacked Calvin James. They struck from the right and left simultaneously, trying to tear the black American to pieces. James flashed his arms in a quick, deceptive motion, while his legs shot out without warning, each boot kicking a leopard-man in the lower abdomen.

James quickly grabbed the wrists of his closest opponent and swung the leopard-man into the second attacker. Cat-killer number two grunted and tumbled to the ground, but the first opponent managed to keep his balance and lashed a kick toward James's groin. The Phoenix warrior blocked the kick with a thigh. He hissed through clenched teeth as the killer's claws raked his leg.

"Son of a bitch!" James cried as he jumped back and assumed a T-dachi fighting stance. "Come on, asshole. Now I'm pissed off!"

The leopard-man raised his clawed fists and watched James, waiting for the American to make the next move. The badass from Chicago raised a boot and snapped the toe forward. Expecting a kick, the leopard-man reached for the leg with his talons, leaving his head unprotected. James punched him in the mouth with a left jab. The guy's head danced backward. James hit him again with a left hook.

The second punch knocked the leopard-man off balance. He started to fall. James kicked him with a powerful heel-kick under the jaw. The kick snapped back the African's head with fearsome force, breaking his neck.

The other leopard-man got to his feet and prepared to attack again. David McCarter, who had finished off his own opponent, turned to help Calvin James. McCarter suddenly grabbed the man from behind and stomped a boot to the back of the African's knee. The killer's leg buckled and he fell to his knees. McCarter tossed the guy's own cape over his head. The leopard-man growled like the beast he imitated as he tried to pull the cape from his face with one claw-studded hand and lash out at McCarter with the other.

A heel-of-the-palm stroke blocked the attacking arm, and McCarter's other palm swatted the African's hand as he tried to move the cape. The blow drove the man's clawed hand into his own face. Sharp steel plunged deep and crimson stained the leopard cape. The African's terrible scream ended in a gasping sob as he fainted.

Rafael Encizo had raised his camera as a leopardman lunged toward him. The Cuban pressed the shutter and a brilliant white flash exploded in the leopardman's face. Blinded by the light, the African killer attempted a wild punch and missed. Encizo deftly kicked him in the balls and smashed the camera over the African's skull.

The dazed leopard-man staggered, but before he fell Encizo seized him and used him as a shield to make a desperate charge toward the lone gunman on the porch. The smiling African aimed his Walther pistol, trying to lock the sights on Encizo's head. The Cuban ran in a zigzag pattern, shifting the stunned leopardman to create a more elusive target. The smile melted from the gunman's face as he pulled the trigger.

A 9 mm slug tore into the neck of the man Encizo was using as a shield. Blood splashed the Cuban warrior's face and shirt as he continued to run forward. The leopard-man's body convulsed in his grasp.

The gunman fired his pistol again, as Encizo, three yards from the porch, heaved the dying man forward.

The second bullet punched through the leopard-man's backbone, and more dead than alive, he collapsed at the porch steps.

The gunman cursed under his breath as he looked around for Encizo. He found him, when the Cuban vaulted over the handrail and crashed into him feet-first. A boot slammed the Walther from the African's fingers, and Encizo's hands found his opponent's throat. The black man, who was larger, grabbed the Cuban's wrists and turned sharply to ram Encizo into the doorjamb.

The Phoenix fighter groaned when his back connected with the hard wood, but he held on to his opponent's throat with one hand and clawed at the guy's eyes with the other. When the African turned his head sharply to avoid having his eyes torn from their sockets, he lost his balance at the same time that Encizo's fingernails raked his cheek. As the thug cried out in pain and alarm, both men toppled across the threshold into the room.

They hit the floor hard, but neither one slackened his effort. Encizo lashed a left hook to the side of his opponent's skull. His knuckles stung from the punch, but the African barely seemed to notice. They began to wrestle. Encizo realized his opponent was bigger, heavier and about ten years younger than he was. The odds favored the African in a wrestling match.

Encizo planted a foot in his opponent's chest and kicked the African away long enough to scramble to his feet. The killer also jumped up and plucked something from his pocket. The familiar click of a switchblade snapping into position warned Encizo of the new threat even before he saw the six-inch steel in the black man's fist.

The African slashed at Encizo's face. The Cuban retreated and backed into a desk in the darkness. His opponent attempted to thrust. As Encizo dodged the attack, he moved around until it was the black man who was closer to the desk. Encizo's foot kicked a tin wastepaper basket as he tried to avoid the dancing steel blade.

"American pig!" the African growled.

"Stupido!" Encizo spit. "I am a Cuban advisor. Chou sent us, you idiot!"

"What?" the African demanded. "I was told nothing of... Liar!"

The black man lunged. Encizo swiftly scooped up the wastebasket for a shield. Steel punctured tin and the knife lodged in the metal container. Encizo shoved hard and drove his opponent off balance. The African fell backward and struck the desk. His body fell heavily to the floor.

An overhead light suddenly came on. Encizo blinked at the unexpected brightness as he turned to see Gary Manning in the doorway. The Canadian's left hand was near the wall switch. His right fist held the African gunman's Walther P-38.

"You okay?" Manning asked. He glanced down at the motionless figure of the man Encizo had fought. "That guy sure isn't."

Blood and gray brain matter stained the corner of the desk and formed a small pool on the floor around the dead man's head. His skull had split when he struck the desk. Encizo barely looked at the corpse. He was glad to be alive and did not regret the death of the man who had tried to kill him.

"This guy knew Chou," Encizo declared. "He told me as much, just before our conversation came to an abrupt end."

"Let's get back to Nairobi," Manning replied. "Maybe we've got enough evidence to convince Mandera that we're finally making some progress."

14

Dr. Julia Kyler leaned over Yakov Katzenelenbogen's shoulder as he ran his fingertips across the dots embossed on the thick paper. Katz was conscious of the weight of Julia's breast against his shoulder and he felt her breath at his neck.

"Okay," Julia said softly, her lips almost touching his ear. "Read it out loud for me, Yakov."

"It's the opening act of Shakespeare's *A Midsummer Night's Dream*," Katz answered. "Theseus and Hippolyta are discussing the upcoming wedding. Aegeus and his daughter Hermia enter, along with Lysander and Demetrius."

"Very good," she assured him. "You're mastering braille very quickly."

"I have something of a knack for languages," Katz said, turning his head slightly. He smelled her perfume and felt the warmth of her face less than an inch from his own. "My father was a linguist and a translator in Europe. I was raised speaking four languages, and..."

"Yes?" she inquired, placing a hand on Katz's shoulder.

"I'm talking too much," he replied. "That's something I really shouldn't do."

"Why not?" Julia asked. "Oh, that's right. You're some sort of cloak-and-dagger expert. Do you have to keep everything secret from me? I'm your doctor, Yakov. We have a code of conduct that includes maintaining confidences as well, you know."

"It's not quite the same," Katz said, aware that her lips were nearly touching his own. "I . . . I appreciate you coming here to help me with braille tonight. I know you're off duty."

"Let's just say you're a special patient, Yakov," she whispered. "I don't mind spending extra time with you."

"I'm so glad," Katz replied.

He turned his head slightly and touched his lips to hers. The kiss was brief and tender. Julia did not move away, and her hand remained on his shoulder. She gazed at his mouth and then at the bandage over his eyes.

Julia leaned forward and returned the kiss. His left arm moved around her waist and drew her closer. Julia's hand slid along his neck and her lips parted. Katz's tongue touched hers. The kiss lingered, the passion increased. Then, frustrated by not facing Julia directly, Katz rose from his chair at the small desk. He slid his left hand up her back, caressing her spine. The stump of his right arm touched her ribs as they kissed.

"I don't know if we should be doing this," Julia whispered, but she sighed as Katz's lips brushed her neck.

"We're not kids, Julia," he said gently. "If you want me to stop, I will."

"I know what I *want* to do, Yakov," she said breathlessly. "I'm just not sure I should."

"If you need more time, I'll understand," Katz assured her, stroking her breast. "I might not like it, but I'll understand."

Julia gasped at the erotic sensation as Katz manipulated her breast with a feather touch. "I don't think I'd like it if we waited, either," she said. "I'm afraid you might change your mind...."

He kissed her again and led her to the bed, moving with ease in the familiar hospital room. Julia sat on the edge of the mattress, and Katz joined her and stroked her back.

"Somebody might come in," she said, not certain she cared.

"There are two bodyguards stationed outside the door to keep people out," Katz said, smiling. "It's about time they earned their pay."

"Too bad we can't lock the door." Julia sighed. "Maybe I should jam a chair against the door or something."

"That would make my watchdogs suspicious," Katz said. "They might be afraid you're trying to strangle me with your stethoscope. Besides, I don't want you to get up. I don't want you to move from this spot, Julia."

His hand found the hem of her skirt. His fingers crept over her knee and caressed her thigh, sliding the skirt higher. Katz kissed her as his hand stroked her thigh. Julia's hands brushed across the crotch of Katz's pajamas.

Slowly they undressed each other. Julia had not been with a man for a long time and she savored Katz's gentle yet passionate touch. He did not rush her, but kissed and caressed her with a loving attention.

Katz relished the touch of the woman he had come to know in darkness. His hand explored her body, eager to know what his eyes could not tell him. The Israeli's mouth glided across her flesh as he covered her body with his. He ached with desire greater than he had known for years, but they made love slowly.

"Would it sound terribly trite if I said you're wonderful?" Katz whispered as he held the woman close to his chest.

"Not at all," Julia assured him. "I hope I don't sound trite if I say... well, I haven't felt like this for a long time. You make me feel young and attractive."

"You're beautiful," he assured her.

"You can't see me," she replied.

"But I'm learning to grope real good," Katz said, smiling.

"You grope just great." Julia giggled. "I... I'm a bit frightened, Yakov."

"Frightened?" he asked, stroking her hair.

"When the bandages come off, you may still be blind," she explained. "When we first met, I was worried about your ability to cope with that."

"I might still be lying on my back feeling sorry for myself if it hadn't been for you," Katz replied. "Now, I'm lying on my back feeling absolutely wonderful."

"That makes two of us," Julia confirmed. "But if you regain your vision, you'll probably go back to the work you've been involved with in the past. That means I'll never see you again...."

"Don't be too sure of that," Katz said as he kissed her forehead.

15

"The airfield was run by some former Rhodesians. They fled to Kenya after the revolution in 1980, when the white ruling class fell out of power and the black majority turned Rhodesia into the republic of Zimbabwe," Captain Mandera explained as he met with Phoenix Force in his office at NSS headquarters. "The terrorists must have thought they were West Europeans or British."

"Yeah," Calvin James said grimly. "We found the bodies when we were looking for the fuel supply tanks at the airstrip. The leopard-men had torn them up pretty badly."

"Incredible," Mandera said, shaking his head. "I saw some of the victims of the terrorists before, but I still hoped that somehow the stories of leopard-men would prove false. Such savage behavior by Africans reinforces the negative image of my brothers that some people have in other parts of the world."

"Savages come in all ethnic groups and nationalities. You can't generalize that way," Gary Manning stated. "We have a German friend who gets upset when someone associates his country with the Nazis.

I'm sure most Arabs don't care to be lumped in with the trigger-happy fanatics who murdered an innocent American and shoved him and his wheelchair off the deck of the *Achille Lauro*."

"The leopard-men are real enough, Mandera," Rafael Encizo said emphatically. "We brought you evidence of that."

"I know," Mandera admitted. "You brought three of them back with you."

"The others are dead and still at the airstrip," David McCarter commented as he fired up a Player's cigarette. "We can question the survivors under the influence of a truth drug, but I don't think they'll tell us any more than we already know."

"Chou and Li are definitely connected with the terrorism," Manning explained. "They may even be the ringleaders of the gang."

"You explained about the Russian helicopter, and your suspicions that some of the men working for the Chinese might be from the Congo," Mandera said with a nod. "But that isn't really solid proof."

"One of the killers at the airfield recognized Chou's name when I claimed he had sent me," Encizo stated. "The two Chinese are involved in this, there's no doubt about that."

"Maybe we'll have some more answers after the tape recording from the limpet microphone has been translated," McCarter suggested. "From what I heard, the conversation after we left the tea plantation was a combination of Chinese and Swahili."

"Chinese, Swahili and Lingala," Sergeant Ngong declared as he entered the office. "We had a hard time getting the tape translated, had to drag a man out of bed to get him down here to work on the tape. There's only one man on our staff who's fluent in Lingala."

"What the hell is Lingala?" Encizo asked.

"A language spoken in Central Africa," Ngong answered, "especially in the Congo. Here's the translation. I think you'll find it interesting."

He handed the transcript to Captain Mandera. The NSS officer scanned the pages, nodding with satisfaction. Then he tensed and turned to Ngong with a frown.

"Are they certain about this translation, Sergeant?" Mandera demanded. He handed the transcript to Calvin James.

"Absolutely," Ngong confirmed. "Pretty scary, isn't it?"

"Yes," Mandera agreed. "And I don't think we should waste time reading it one at a time. Chou and Li talked about your visit, gentlemen. They were suspicious, but not certain if you were enemies or just the over-zealous amateur film crew you appeared to be. Then they gave their men orders to carry out an attack on the American embassy here in Nairobi tonight. The killers are supposed to leave as soon as their comrades return from the airfield."

"That means the leopard-men at the airfield weren't sent to kill us," McCarter mused. "We just happened to land at the site of their most recent hit."

"The most recent hit is going to be at the embassy," James corrected, reading through the transcript. "I hope it's not too late to stop them."

"When the guys from the airfield don't return," Manning commented as he headed for the door, "they'll try to contact the hit squad by radio."

"Unless they've got a frequency for the next world, that isn't going to do them much good," McCarter said, following Manning out the door.

"So they'll either scratch the mission at the embassy or go ahead without the missing members," Encizo added. He stepped into the corridor behind the British and Canadian commandos.

"We'd better assume they do the latter," James remarked. He glanced at his wristwatch and noted it was 1:22 a.m.

The headquarters building of the National Security Service was all but deserted at that hour. Phoenix Force hurried through the empty corridors, followed by Mandera. Ngong slipped past the others and took a key-ring from his belt to unlock the door to the arms room.

"I might be able to get some troops from the parachute regiment to assist us," Mandera announced.

"There's no time for that," Gary Manning answered. "It would take too long to explain our strategy to the paratroopers, and I doubt that they've been trained to handle this kind of terrorist situation."

"There's also the problem of taking action on foreign soil," Encizo added. "I don't think you'll be able to get authorization to send Kenyan troops onto embassy property. We'll have to handle this pretty much on our own.''

Ngong opened the arms room and headed for a steel locker. He opened a thick security lock and stepped aside to allow Phoenix Force to select weapons and equipment. Ngong unlocked a gun rack and removed two Sterling MK-4 submachine guns assigned to himself and Captain Mandera. The NSS officer signed the log and wrote in the serial numbers as Phoenix Force chose their weapons for the night assignment.

Gary Manning, the best rifle marksman of the unit, selected an FN FAL assault rifle with a Starlite night scope and attached a foot-long sound-suppressor to the threaded barrel. He slipped into a shoulder holster and shoved an Israeli-made Desert Eagle into the leather under his arm. The big semiauto pistol packed a .357 Magnum wallop, and others like it had saved Manning's life on several occasions. The demolitions pro also donned a compact backpack that contained C-4 plastic explosives—just in case.

Calvin James chose an M-16 assault rifle and slid into a Jackass leather holster rig with a .45 caliber Colt Commander under his left arm and a Jet-Aer G-96 fighting dagger in a scabbard under his right. The Phoenix Force medic also carried a well-stocked first-aid kit at the small of his back.

With an appreciative smile as he recognized his favorite weapons, David McCarter armed himself with a 9 mm Ingram MAC-10 with a foot-long silencer attached and a Browning Hi-Power autoloader of the same caliber. The Briton also selected a Barnett Commando crossbow with a skeletal metal stock and a cocking lever and he hung a quiver of crossbow bolts on his left hip.

Rafael Encizo carried even more weapons. In addition to his Heckler & Koch 9 mm machine pistol, the Cuban buckled on a gunbelt with a Smith & Wesson M-59 9 mm double-action automatic in a hip holster. A Cold Steel Tanto fighting knife was attached to the belt in a cross-draw position. Encizo also carried a Walther PPK in shoulder leather, with three *shaken* throwing stars attached to the straps. Finally, the Cuban clipped a Gerber Mark I combat dagger to the top of his boot.

"I wish we had time to change clothes," James remarked. "These khakis don't blend into the darkness as well as black camouflage fatigues."

"A disadvantage against the enemy," Manning agreed. "But at least it should prevent the Marines guarding the embassy from mistaking us as enemy invaders and opening fire on us."

"Do you think the leopard-men will actually attack, or will other terrorists in ordinary clothes just lob grenades at the American embassy the way they did at the Soviets?" Mandera inquired, checking the chambers of his Smith & Wesson revolver.

"It could go either way," Encizo replied, as he loaded extra magazines into the ammo pouches on his belt. "Originally, Chou and Li planned to send in the cat-man killers, because they were waiting for those guys to come back from the airstrip. But they might try just about anything.''

"Trying to second-guess terrorists is a waste of time," McCarter added. "They don't think like trained soldiers, and many of them are downright irrational."

"Then I'm surprised that you can't second-guess them with ease, David," Manning said with a grin as he passed out an assortment of tear gas and SAS flash-bang grenades. McCarter didn't deign to answer the good-natured gibe.

"These concussion blasters can be pretty indiscriminate," James commented. "They can take out innocent people as easily as enemies."

"But the blast is seldom fatal," Encizo added, taking four M-17 protective masks from the locker. "We'd better take these in case we need to use tear gas."

"Let's quit talking about it and get to work, damn it," McCarter said impatiently, sliding the sling of his MAC-10 onto his shoulder.

"I can't argue with that," Manning agreed.

16

Two Marines emerged from the side entrance of the United States embassy at the corner of Haile Selassie Avenue. A staff sergeant and a corporal, the pair patrolled the grounds to make certain the Marines on duty were alert. Since the violence at the Soviet embassy, the Marine guards at the American post had increased security.

The NCO of the guard mount carried a clipboard under his arm and a pistol in a button-flap holster on his hip. The sidearm was not loaded, although the sergeant carried a magazine for it in an ammo pouch on his belt. Official military policy required guard units to carry unloaded guns unless patrolling an area recognized as a combat zone.

The Marines in Beirut in 1983 had carried empty rifles when a terrorist drove a truck bomb into their barracks. Two hundred and forty-one Marines were killed. Kenya was hardly Lebanon, but the Marines would have felt a lot better if they had been authorized to load their weapons. The sergeant glanced around the grounds, unable to locate the guards.

"Where the hell are they?" the NCO rasped, reaching for the Colt 1911A1 on his hip. "If they're fuckin' off, I'll have their assholes hangin' from the flagpole."

"I'm not so sure that's what's happened, Sergeant," the corporal replied, wishing he had a weapon.

"Maybe not," the sergeant said as he slid a seven-round mag into the butt-well of the Colt. He worked the slide to jack the first 230-grain hard-ball .45 cartridge into the chamber. "Stay here and watch. If I get in any trouble, don't be a goddamn hero. Head back to Lieutenant Jackson on the double."

The NCO walked toward a cluster of bushes, pistol at the ready. He noticed a familiar object on the ground. It was a white "flying saucer" hat, the service cap worn with the Marine Corps dress blues, the regular uniform of the day for embassy guard personnel. The sergeant stooped to pick up the cap. Something wet stained the bill.

"Blood," the Marine whispered, unable to repress a cold shudder that slithered up his spine.

The bushes suddenly exploded with violent movement, and two figures leaped forward. The sergeant glimpsed leopard fur and nightmare faces with dark human features topped by spotted cat-head masks. The sergeant raised his pistol. Steel claws snapped shut around his wrist like a bear trap. Talons punctured flesh and splintered bone.

The sergeant screamed, and blood squirted from the severed artery in his wrist. The pistol tumbled from his twitching fingers. The clawed hands of the second leopard-man seized the Marine's neck and adroitly ripped out his throat. The sergeant crumpled to the ground, crimson splashing his blue tunic.

"Oh, Christ!" the corporal exclaimed as he turned and ran for the building.

A silenced pistol coughed harshly. Two 9 mm bullets struck the Marine corporal between the shoulder blades. He crashed to the ground, groaning as blood rose into his throat and mouth. A terrible weight descended on the wounded Marine's back. Steel claws gripped his head, and sharp metal punched through the fragile bone at his temples. The Marine felt a split second of incredible pain before he plunged into the endless realm of death.

More leopard-men emerged from the bushes, accompanied by other African killers dressed in black and armed with silenced pistols. The invaders crept toward the embassy. Some moved outside the building, others pushed through the side door and silently entered.

On the street, near the embassy, a large, three-ton military-style truck was parked. Two nervous Africans sat inside the cab, straining their eyes to try to watch their comrades inside the fenced compound. The driver struck a match for a cigarette. He dropped it in his lap when he saw two men point submachine guns at the windshield.

Captain Mandera held his MK-4 in one fist and raised his open ID folder in his other hand. Sergeant Ngong stood near the officer and gestured with his Sterling subgun, signaling for the men in the truck to get out of the vehicle.

The driver turned the key in the ignition, planning to ram the two security officers. His hand moved to the gear shift. Hard steel jammed into the side of his neck. The steel cylinder pushed under the driver's jawbone as his fingers froze on the stick shift.

Rafael Encizo stood on the running board of the truck with his S&W pistol thrust through the open window, muzzle held against the driver's jaw. "If this truck moves, I'll blow your brains out," he said in a menacing tone.

The man seated beside the driver slipped a hand between his legs for the Tokarev pistol hidden under his thigh. The barrel of a Colt Commander appeared at the other window and poked the guy behind the right ear.

"Scratch your nuts later," Calvin James ordered as he shoved the gun muzzle against the man's skull. "Put your hands on the dashboard until I tell you otherwise."

The doors of a Volkswagen Beetle parked behind the truck popped open and two Africans jumped out. One held an Uzi submachine gun and the other pulled a Browning pistol from his belt, both prepared to get rid of Encizo, James and the two NSS agents.

Neither lived to aim their guns at the targets, let alone pull the triggers. David McCarter's silencer-equipped Ingram MAC-10 snarled, and three 9 mm rounds ripped through the chest of the guy with the Uzi. The pistol-packing terrorist died just as fast when Gary Manning nailed him with a trio of 7.62 mm slugs directly through the heart. The Canadian watched the pair fall dead and lowered his FAL rifle. Smoke drifted from the muzzle of the sound-suppressor attached to the barrel.

Encizo and James dragged the two terrorists from the truck and shoved them against the hood. Mandera and Ngong took charge of the prisoners while the four men of Phoenix Force headed for the U.S. embassy.

Six members of the enemy hit team had remained outside the building to cover the lawn. Two of them heard strange noises in the street where the getaway vehicles were waiting, but the noise was faint and they could not be certain what they had heard. The moan of a dying man? The sputtering report of a silenced weapon? Had they imagined the sounds? Had they heard the fighting within the embassy and incorrectly thought the sounds came from the street? Or...

One of them peered between the bars of the fence. He saw two of his comrades by the truck being handcuffed by Sergeant Ngong while Captain Mandera covered the pair with his MK-4 subgun. The terrorist also saw the dead gunmen beside the VW. He did not see Phoenix Force and did not realize that his face had appeared in the center of the cross hairs of a Starlite night scope.

Gary Manning squeezed the trigger of his FAL. The silenced rifle coughed, and a high-velocity 7.62 mm round smashed into the bridge of the terrorist's nose. The bullet knifed through the skull cavity and rearranged the man's brains before blasting an exit hole at the back of his head.

The terrorist next to the slain invader gasped with surprise and terror as his comrade fell dead right in front of him. The guy opened his mouth to shout a warning to his other teammates. David McCarter fired his crossbow at that precise instant.

The bolt sizzled through the bars and shot into the terrorist's open mouth. The steel point burst through the base of his skull. His teeth clamped around the shaft as fiberglass split and released a lethal dose of cyanide. The poison was redundant, because the man was already dead before it could take effect.

Encizo hit the fence first. The muscular Cuban grabbed the iron bars and pulled himself up, bracing his feet against the metal surface to assist his climb to the top. He noticed two terrorists jogging across the lawn toward the fence. Encizo swung to the ground on the other side as the enemy raised their weapons.

Calvin James poked his M-16 between the bars and fired at the two gunmen. A trio of 5.56 mm slugs hissed from the foot-long sound-suppressor and ripped into the torso of the closest terrorist. The man tumbled to the lawn as his comrade dropped to one knee and aimed his R-4 rifle at James. But the American commando had already shifted the aim of his M-16 and triggered the rifle before his opponent could fire a shot. Two bullets smashed through the forehead of the terrorist and blew off the top of his skull.

Another gunman appeared from the bushes and fired a Beretta M-12 submachine gun at Calvin James. The Phoenix pro dropped to the ground as 9 mm slugs rang against iron bars. The Beretta roared and spit flame from its unshielded muzzle. The muzzle-flash illuminated the terrorist's fierce features as he sprayed the fence with full-auto fury.

Encizo triggered his H&K MP-5 and blasted a trio of 9 mm slugs into the side of the enemy gunman's head. The terrorist's skull exploded like a grisly volcano of blood and gory brain matter. The Beretta blaster fell from the assassin's grasp, and his mangled corpse fell to earth.

David McCarter discarded the Barnett crossbow and climbed the iron fence. Encizo covered him from within the embassy grounds while James and Manning watched from the opposite side of the fence, rifles held ready. McCarter leaped to the embassy lawn. James followed and then Manning scaled the wall.

The report of unmuted gunfire had alerted the other terrorists to danger. Two gunmen ran from the back door. Others appeared from both sides of the building.

"Looks like the shit has definitely hit the fan," James remarked as he raised the M-16 to his shoulder and pumped three 5.56 mm rounds into the chest of an opponent.

Manning's FAL picked off another terrorist at the corner of the embassy building. Surviving terrorists ducked behind cover. Phoenix Force advanced, "leapfrogging"—one man darting to cover while the others guarded his progress, then another man moving forward and so on.

A terrorist at the doorway sprayed a hasty volley of Uzi slugs at Phoenix Force. The bullets raked the shrubbery behind the commandos without coming close to them. The ultraprofessionals did not waste ammo shooting blindly. The Uzi-wielding thug mistakenly thought he had succeeded in pinning down the four warriors.

"Hapa!" he cried to his comrades. *"Hapa!"*

Two more gunmen ventured into the open, weapons at the ready as they scanned the area for the Phoenix crusaders. They found them as the four fighters opened fire. Full-auto slugs slashed into the flesh of the careless terrorists. Their bodies jerked and twisted violently from the impact of high-velocity projectiles that pulverized vital organs. The guy with the Uzi and his two bold comrades collapsed and their life fluids leaked into the ground.

Calvin James yanked the pin from a tear-gas grenade and expertly pitched it through the open doorway while Manning fired a trio of FAL rounds across the threshold to discourage the enemy from tossing the canister back out the door. At the same time,

McCarter and Encizo lobbed concussion grenades at the terrorists stationed at the sides of the building.

The explosions erupted almost simultaneously, the blasts rolling together into one great roar. Phoenix Force charged forward. Encizo fired his MP-5 at the doorway while Manning pulled the pin from a flash-bang grenade and lobbed it across the threshold. The Cuban and Canadian warriors moved to the sides of the doorway and stood clear of the opening as the grenade exploded, then they donned gas masks and plunged inside. McCarter and James separated to cover the sides of the building.

Several bodies were sprawled across the floor of the hallway within the embassy. Many of these were dazed terrorists, not dead but rendered insensible by the concussion blast. Others were slain Marines, their bodies mutilated by the savage claws of leopard-men. Three terrorists, including a man dressed in a leopard cape with fresh blood on his steel talons, were still on their feet. They staggered like drunkards, disoriented by the concussion blast and choking on tear gas.

Encizo stepped forward and backhanded the frame of his H&K across the face of the first terrorist. The man fell unconscious as another thug made a clumsy grab for Encizo, half-blind from the effects of the tear gas. The Cuban easily dodged the groping enemy and whipped a backfist to the guy's face. The man fell backward and hit a wall. Manning moved in and knocked him out with a hard left hook.

The leopard-man staggered away from the commandos. The blood on the man's claws, blood that had been torn from the veins of American Marines, enraged Encizo. He swiftly pulled a *shaken* from the harness of his shoulder rig and hurled it at the fleeing terrorist. The steel throwing star struck the leopard-man between the shoulder blades. He screamed and turned around, arms flapping in a desperate effort to dislodge the sharp metal from his back.

Encizo's arm snapped forward and unleashed another *shaken* star. The steel projectile hit the leopard-man in the center of the chest. Sharp tines split his sternum. Overwhelmed by shock and pain, he dropped to the floor.

Gunshots echoed inside the building. Although several Marines had been murdered by the invaders, others had been alerted to the danger in time to load their weapons and face the terrorists on more even terms. Most of the invaders armed with firearms had already been slain by Phoenix Force and the few that remained were not as well trained as the embassy guard force. The leopard-men soon discovered that steel claws were no match for bullets.

Three panicked terrorists managed to escape out the front door of the embassy, but they did not get down the marble steps alive. David McCarter was waiting for them. He cut down the fanatics with a merciless volley of Ingram slugs. The trio convulsed in a wild dance of death, splashing each other with blood before their corpses tumbled down the stairs.

As Calvin James crouched near the side of the building, a second-story window burst apart. Glass showered the ground near the black warrior. He ducked and crept to the wall for shelter. At the sound of an object striking the earth, he turned to see the blood-drenched corpse of a leopard man sprawled on the grass.

"Hold it, motherfucker!" a voice shouted from the window above.

James glanced up. A Marine sergeant leaned out the window with a .45 in his fist, pointed at the Phoenix pro. James stepped back to allow the Marine to get a better look at him.

"So keep your mother off the street, jar head," James called back with a wide grin. "We gonna threaten each other or we gonna kick ass, man?"

"You're on our side?" the sergeant asked with a frown.

"I'm not wearing a pussycat coat," James replied. "Three of my buddies are here, too. Tell your other Marine buddies not to shoot us down by—"

Another window exploded, this time on the first floor. A leopard-man bounded outside and charged straight at James, clawed fists raised for action. James lifted his M-16 to block the attack. The steel frame met the leopard-man's talons, but the terrorist's momentum knocked James off balance.

The Phoenix pro did not try to right himself, but folded a leg and fell backward, raising a boot to meet the belly of his opponent. When James straightened his knee he sent the leopard-man hurtling head over heels in a judo circle-throw. Though the terrorist hit the ground hard, he quickly scrambled to his feet. James rolled on his belly, M-16 aimed at the killer.

Two shots cracked from the second story. Big .45 slugs tore chunks of flesh from the leopard-man's chest. The terrorist stumbled and fell dead. James glanced up at the Marine NCO, who was still pointing his Colt at the fanatic's corpse.

"Quit lyin' around, damn it!" the Marine snapped. "We got work to do, fella."

INSIDE THE EMBASSY, Rafael Encizo kicked open a door to an office. He stood clear of the doorway as two pistol shots cracked from the room within. The Cuban poked his H&K machine pistol around the edge and opened fire. He prayed the gunman was not a Marine or a member of the embassy staff protecting himself against terrorists, but Encizo could not afford to peek inside first to see who was there.

Three terrorists lurked within. An African thug sat on the floor with two 9 mm holes in his chest. His Makarov pistol lay near his lifeless fingers. The two surviving terrorists were clad in leopard-man costumes. One lunged for Encizo, apparently unconcerned about the MP-5 blaster in his fists.

Encizo squeezed the trigger. A single 9 mm slug, the last in the Cuban's H&K, burned into the leopard-man's solar plexus. The terrorist screamed in pain and fury, but he kept coming and lashed out with the claws on both hands.

One steel-taloned fist struck at Encizo's face. He turned his head abruptly to avoid the stroke. Claws raked the M-17 gas mask, ripping it from Encizo's face. The other set of steel "fingers" hit the MP-5 and yanked the empty weapon from Encizo's grasp. The Phoenix pro responded with a powerful karate kick that sent the wounded terrorist staggering across the room and broke the bottom rib on his left side.

The second leopard-man did not retreat or surrender, but launched himself at Encizo and slashed a claw at the Cuban's head. Encizo dodged the attack and reached for the hilt of his Cold Steel Tanto. The leopard-man swung a cross-body claw stroke for Encizo's throat as the six-inch blade rose to meet the attack. Sharp steel cut deep into the terrorist's wrist and blood jetted from the severed artery. The African screamed. Encizo slashed the side of his left hand across the nape of his opponent's neck.

Stunned and injured, the leopard-man staggered away from Encizo, but the Cuban moved with him and drove the Tanto into the terrorist's chest with a powerful upward thrust. The heavy blade punched through rib bone and sank into the fanatic's heart.

Encizo left the Tanto in his opponent's chest and shoved the dying man aside. He turned just as the first leopard-man, severely wounded, crawled toward the discarded Makarov on the floor. The steel talons of the fanatic's glove-weapons hindered him from picking up the Russian-made pistol.

The Cuban drew his Walther PPK from leather, snapped off the safety catch and fired two 7.65 mm bullets into the leopard-man's face. The terrorist collapsed across the floor, a crimson pool oozing from his smashed features. Encizo wearily returned the Walther to its shoulder holster and stooped to retrieve his Heckler & Koch machine pistol.

Then he noticed a sinister object in the far corner of the room. A large bundle of dark cylinders were bound together with wire. Blasting caps had been inserted among the dynamite sticks and wired to an electric timing mechanism. Encizo realized he was holding his breath and consciously exhaled.

"Gary!" the Cuban shouted. "You'd better get in here!"

The Cuban approached the bomb and examined it. At first glance, the device looked simple, and Encizo thought he might be able to deactivate it by merely cutting the connecting wires. But when he looked more closely he realized the wiring was more complex than he had first thought. A cord linked the main wiring with something in the center of the dynamite sticks.

"Don't touch it!" Gary Manning said sharply as he appeared in the doorway.

"Don't worry," Encizo answered, happily stepping aside to let Manning deal with the time bomb.

The Phoenix Force demolitions expert knelt by the explosives and carefully studied the wiring. He reached inside his shirt and removed a small leather packet. He unzipped it and removed small wire cutters and a thin wooden probe. Then he took a penlight from his pocket and looked closely at the cord that extended from the core of the dynamite.

"What we have here is a simple contraption to detonate the explosives if the wires are disconnected," Manning explained as he peered between the dynamite sticks with the aid of the penlight. "This cord runs to a shutter-style trigger mechanism, which is attached to a tubular explosive in the center. I think it's a magnesium flare, rigged to go off when the wiring is tampered with—"

"Freeze, you assholes!" a voice shouted from the door.

A young Marine second lieutenant aimed a .45 Colt at the Phoenix Force pair. Two PFCs backed up the officer, pointing their M-16 rifles at Encizo and Manning. All three seemed nervous and unsure of how to handle the situation.

"Get up and put your hands on your heads," the lieutenant ordered. "Try anything and we'll blow your ass away!"

"We'll all get our butts blown away if you don't let me finish deactivating this bomb," Manning replied, barely glancing up at the Marines.

"The timer says we've got sixty seconds," Encizo added. "You'd better listen to him, fellas."

"Looks to me like he's putting that thing together," the shave-tail lieutenant declared, but he was still reluctant to open fire.

"So shoot me, kid," Manning remarked as he inserted his wooden probe into the center of the dynamite. "If you won't let me deactivate this thing it won't make any difference anyway."

"What's going on, Lieutenant?" a Marine major demanded as he marched down the hall. A barrel-chested man with a bull neck, the major carried a pistol in one hand and a broken chair leg in the other. He had used both weapons to dispatch four terrorists during the battle.

"We found these two suspicious characters, sir," the junior officer answered. "I don't know if they're enemies or not...."

"Step aside," the major demanded. He stared at Manning and Encizo. "You know a couple other fellas who were killing these bastards outside the embassy?"

"A tall black guy and a deranged Briton," Encizo confirmed.

"That's them," the major said with a nod. "What are you doing? Is that a bomb?"

"In ten more seconds it's going to be a funeral for about half the people in this building," Manning growled as he slid the wire cutters inside the dynamite bundle. "Call your people to stop pointing guns at me. It makes me nervous."

"Put that weapon away, Lieutenant," the major ordered. "Are you sure you can disconnect that explosive, mister?"

"We'll know in about five seconds," Manning answered as he moved the cutters to the main wiring.

The Canadian clipped the first wire. He sighed with relief and cut the next one. The clippers snapped shut on the last wire as the time clicked to zero.

A buzzer signaled that the time was up.

"That's it," Manning announced.

A cheer erupted from the corridor, where several Marines had assembled. Manning ignored them as he cut the wires holding the dynamite sticks together. He parted the sticks and removed the magnesium flare. The Canadian calmly pulled the Number Six blasting caps from the individual sticks of dynamite.

"Now that the crisis is over," the major began gruffly, "who the hell are you people and where the hell did you come from? If you knew the embassy was going to be attacked, why the fuck didn't you warn us in advance so the bastards wouldn't have caught us with our pants down?"

"Check with the deputy ambassador about that," Encizo told him. "A fellow named Jerome Tompkins. Captain Mandera of the Kenyan National Security Service did call the embassy to warn them that terrorists had targeted this building for attack. Tompkins hung up without replying. Mandera called back on his car phone on our way over here. Tompkins said something about 'stupid crank calls' before he hung up again.''

"Son-of-a-bitch," the major said grimly. "Where the hell is Tompkins?"

"I think he's in the office next door," a corporal answered, tilting his head toward the right. "Should I get him for you, sir?"

"*I'll* get *him*," the major replied, putting his pistol away. He kept the chair leg handy as he moved toward the door. "Somebody call an ambulance. Tompkins is gonna need it."

"You do what you want with Tompkins, Major," Gary Manning told him. "But you'll have to mop up here and handle the reports without us."

"What the hell is this Lone Ranger shit?" the officer demanded. "Where the hell do you think you're going?"

"We've got some more work to do tonight," Encizo explained. "The terrorists who hit this embassy were just one tentacle of a giant killer octopus. We still have to take out the head."

"Want some company?" the major inquired with a grin.

"Thanks for the offer," Manning replied. "But we can't use you or any of your men for security reasons. Maybe next time."

"I hope so," the major said with a nod. "You go find the rest of those fuckers and kick a few asses for me."

17

Li Yuann opened his fist to show Chou Ziyang the tiny transistors inside a metal disk no larger than a silver dollar. Chou frowned as he stared at the contraption. They had found the disk under the belly of one of the helicopters.

"The device is a transmitter," Li told his comrade. "It is a sophisticated listening device that serves as a wireless microphone and a transmitter. It's difficult to say how far the transmissions would be projected. Perhaps only two or three kilometers. Perhaps twice that distance."

"The Briton must have planted it under the helicopter," Chou said with a sigh. "A pity. He was a fellow pilot. I enjoyed talking to him."

"He is a spy," Li stated. "They were all spies and enemies. With this device they must have heard us discussing the attack on the American embassy."

"I doubt that any of them understands Mandarin Chinese," Chou said. "Let alone Lingala."

"Professionals would have tape-recorded the conversation," Li insisted. "And they were definitely professionals. This listening device isn't the sort of equipment amateurs would use. I think we know what happened to our team at the embassy. They won't be coming back, comrade. Instead, our enemies will soon be coming for us."

"They'll need time to assemble an assault force and they'll have to plan their strategy," Chou stated. But he realized how empty these reassurances were even as he spoke.

"We don't know who's involved in this action," Li said. "Probably the CIA, assisted by the Kenyan government. British Intelligence may also be involved, or even the KGB. We can't remain here."

"Chairman Mao said, 'Oppose war with war,'" Chou declared. "We must not surrender the fight."

"The odds are too great," Li warned. "The chairman also said 'To take the offensive before you are ready is adventurism.' It is time for us to retreat and set up operations again."

"We're creating a revolution," Chou claimed. "'Oppose counterrevolution with revolution.' Mao speaks to us again from his book. He tells us to continue the revolution to crush the enemy."

"We shall continue the revolution," Li promised. "We have fought the revolution for more than two decades, comrade. Our own people in our own land may have abandoned the cause, but we have never swayed from the true path."

"We carried signs and banners," Chou recalled. "We destroyed literature that did not serve the party, and dispatched or punished enemies of the state.

Those things were good, but they are past. Here in Kenya, we have a chance to conquer an entire nation for Maoism, to begin the climb back to power for the only true and just revolution for equality among all classes."

"But we can't continue in this location," Li insisted, trying to repress his impatience. "We'll set up again somewhere else, but we have to survive to do anything—"

"I beg your pardon," an African henchman began as he appeared in the doorway of the two Chinese fanatics' office. "Our radar has located a large object headed this way. It isn't fast enough to be a jet plane, but it is definitely headed this way."

"Sounds like a helicopter." Chou smiled. "It will truly be wonderful if those four scum are stupid enough to return."

"The spy chopper may be an isolated incident," Li said. "Let us not be careless now."

"Protecting our cause is more important than a few lives inside an aircraft," Chou replied. "We can't take any chances. How close is this mystery aircraft?"

"Eight kilometers away," answered the African, a Congolese trooper familiar with aircraft and radar equipment. "We could take up our choppers and force them to land."

"No need for that," Chou replied. "We have three RPG-7 rocket launchers, correct? If the helicopter continues to advance, we will simply take it out with these projectiles."

"Very well, Comrade Chou," the Congolese agreed. He saluted and marched from the main house.

"We can shoot down this lone helicopter," Li remarked. "But they have other aircraft and many times more people on their side."

"Tell the others to start preparing for an emergency evacuation," Chou finally agreed. "If we must, we will cross the border into Uganda and make further plans once we know how big this threat really is."

"Wise decision, Comrade," Li said with a nod.

THE SEAHAWK HELICOPTER hovered just beyond the boundary of the tea plantation. A Kenyan pilot handled the controls. Captain Mandera had finally found someone to fly the chopper so that all four Phoenix Force members could engage the enemy on the ground. Their weapons included every item they had carried into combat at the embassy, plus fragmentation grenades and an M-203 grenade launcher attached to the underside of the barrel of Calvin James's M-16 assault rifle.

The commandos, clad in black night camouflage uniforms, jumped from the hovering aircraft. Their free-fall was brief, as each man waited just long enough to be certain he was clear of the Seahawk before pulling his rip cord. Black parachutes burst from their packs, and the Phoenix pros floated safely to earth.

They landed in a clearing beside a field of tea plants. There was little wind that night which enabled them to avoid one of the dangers of night jumps—being blown off course to land in trees or other solid, unyielding objects.

The Seahawk continued to hover at the outskirts of the plantation, following instructions from Phoenix Force. The veteran combat professionals had considered the possibility that the enemy might have radar and weapons capable of taking out the helicopter if they thought it was a threat. Manning and Encizo carried walkie-talkies to stay in contact with the pilot.

Captain Mandera and Sergeant Ngong were still aboard the Seahawk. The National Security Service agents had wanted to assist Phoenix Force in the final phase of their mission, but neither man was properly trained or experienced enough to take on the terrorists directly. Phoenix Force had planned an assault that required a backup role for Mandera and Ngong without exposing them to extraordinary dangers.

Phoenix Force entered the tea field and slithered through the dense forest of tall plant stalks. They realized that radar might have told the enemy of their approach. That was a calculated risk, one that was part of their job.

They crept through acres of tea plants, straining their eyes and ears for any warning of enemy activity. As they approached the other end of the field, the chirping of insects ahead of them suddenly ceased. Phoenix Force stopped moving to avoid rustling plant stalks and tall grass. They listened intently and peered between the tea plants, searching for the reason why the insects had discontinued their monotonous night songs.

Then lights flashed. The growl of an engine accompanied the rumble of heavy tires treading across earth. Phoenix Force moved forward cautiously as the sounds drew closer. Near the edge of the field, they saw the source.

A dark pickup truck and a Land Rover had driven from the heart of the plantation. Three black men rode in the back of the truck, armed with an assortment of automatic rifles. The Rover contained three men, one positioned behind a RPD 7.62 mm light machine gun mounted at the rear of the vehicle. The RPD was equipped with a drum magazine that contained 100 rounds of ammo.

"Moja kwa moja!" an African in the Rover called out as he pointed at the tea plants. *"Sasa upesi!"*

The machine gunner swung the RPD at the tea field and opened fire. Flame jetted from the barrel as high-velocity slugs raked the plants. Stalks split in two. Leathery tea leaves spit into the air. Phoenix Force flattened themselves on their bellies as sheets of bullets knifed the air overhead.

Encizo saw movement from the corner of his eye. He turned his head slightly and stared into the open jaws of a beast with gray fur, very sharp teeth and a thick snout. It stood less than a foot from his face, its eyes flashing.

The close range made the animal seem larger than it truly was. It resembled a badger, but Encizo did not think badgers were native to Africa. Suddenly, he realized it was a ratel, or honey badger. The small omnivorous beast is feared by many Africans who believe it likes to bite off a man's testicles while he sleeps.

Encizo figured the tale was bullshit, but he did not care to curl up with the ratel to find out. He curled back his lips to expose his teeth and hissed at the animal. The ratel snapped with defiance, then scurried into the tea stalks and vanished.

The enemy machine gun delivered another deadly salvo, trying to drive Phoenix Force into the open. The second volley was aimed lower. Bullets plowed into the ground near Calvin James's position. The black commando ducked his head when clods of dirt spattered his face. A few seconds later he looked up again and peered between the plant trunks. The three guys from the back of the pickup had climbed from their vehicle and were about to add the full-auto fire of their weapons to the hail of bullets.

James knew they would not go away of their own accord so he decided to make them leave—permanently. He rolled on his side and awkwardly aimed his M-16 at the Land Rover, estimating the distance and the trajectory of the missile he planned to launch at the enemy.

He triggered the M-203 grenade launcher. The weapon attachment recoiled violently and caused the Sixteen to jerk in James's fists. A 40 mm grenade burst from the big muzzle of the launcher. The projectile sailed through the remaining tea plants and slammed into the Land Rover.

The grenade exploded on impact. The Rover burst into a brilliant mini-star and chunks of metal, human remains and flaming gasoline flew in all directions. Fiery debris showered the fields. Grass ignited and began to burn. The thick green stems and the tough leathery leaves of the tea plants would not burn quickly, but columns of dense smoke filled the area.

The explosion also convinced the other gunmen to retreat behind the cover of the pickup. One man was not quick enough. Gary Manning tracked the terrorist through the sights of his FAL rifle, then triggered his weapon and blasted three 7.62 mm slugs into the back of the gunman's skull.

The man's corpse sprawled face-first across the ground. The remaining terrorists opened fire with their assault rifles, but they fired blindly, unsure where the Phoenix fighters were located. The heavy smoke reduced visibility for the participants on both sides of the battle.

Another terrorist emerged from the cab of the truck. He yanked the pin from a grenade and prepared to hurl it into the tea crop. However, David McCarter had managed to crawl on his stomach to the edge of the field and saw the goon about to lob an explosive egg at Phoenix Force. The Briton quickly raised his Barnett crossbow and squeezed the trigger just in time.

The bolt sliced through the air and struck the terrorist, its steel tip burrowing deep into the man's flesh. McCarter had been forced to aim and fire so hastily that the shot lacked the Briton's usual pinpoint accuracy. The projectile hit the terrorist high, piercing his shoulder instead of his chest. The man cried out and dropped the grenade, which rolled beyond reach under the truck.

The wounded terrorist fell to his knees as cyanide from the poisoned fiberglass shaft began to ooze into his bloodstream. But before he died from cyanide poisoning, the grenade exploded and the blast killed him instantly.

The dead man was luckier than his comrades. The explosion of the thermite charge blasted the truck from beneath and tipped it over on its side, engulfing the vehicle in burning liquid. The flames enveloped the terrorists pinned under the truck. They shrieked in agony and literally swallowed fire, which scorched their throats and lungs. The terrorists suffocated before the liquid hell could consume flesh, bone and vital organs.

Gary Manning raised the antenna of his walkie-talkie as he staggered from among the tea plants, coughing violently from the pungent smoke. McCarter and Encizo followed him from the burning plants and James was right behind them, wiping his teary eyes and feeding a fresh cartridge grenade into the breech of the M-203.

"Groundstrike to Nighthawk," Manning spoke into the radio. "Nighthawk, come in. Over."

The pilot of the Seahawk did not reply. Again Manning pressed the transmit button and spoke into the radio. "Nighthawk, do you read me?" the Canadian demanded. "The shooting and explosions were not a signal to advance. Do you read me? Over."

Encizo also tried to contact the chopper.

"Groundstrike calling Nighthawk," the Cuban spoke into his walkie-talkie. "Do not advance at this time. Repeat: Do not advance. Over."

The amplified eggbeater whirl of rotor blades drew the warriors' eyes to the night sky above. The Seahawk was heading straight for the heart of the plantation. Either the pilot had failed to get their message or he had chosen to ignore it.

"If Chou and Li have their shit together," Calvin James said grimly, "they'll take that bird out of the sky like a big clay pigeon at a trap shoot."

"Not if we stop 'em first," Manning said as he shoved his radio into its leather case. "Let's do it."

18

"Angalia!" an African terrorist shouted as the Seahawk approached the plantation. *"Angalia!"*

Several of his comrades heeded the warning and ran for cover. The terrorists had been distracted by the gunshots and explosions in the tea fields and had failed to notice the helicopter until the Seahawk was flying across the plantation property. A number of enemy gunmen raised their weapons and opened fire, but most were armed with short-range machine pistols. The bullets failed to reach the Seahawk as the sliding door of the craft rolled open.

Sergeant Ngong knelt behind a British L7A2 general-purpose machine gun mounted at the door. The Kenyan NCO was strapped in by a shoulder harness as he aimed the formidable weapon at the enemy below and triggered the L7A2, firing the powerful 7.62 mm slugs at 750 rounds per minute.

Bullets tore into five terrorists, puncturing their torsos like ice-pick blades through putty. The thugs howled in agony and crumpled to the ground as the survivors ran for cover. The pilot swung the chopper to the west and Ngong fired another salvo at the enemies below. Slugs punched into the metal doors of a Land Rover that two terrorists were using for cover. High-velocity projectiles shattered the windshield and the other windows. Bullets pierced the interior and slammed into the dashboard.

"Watch out!" Captain Mandera shouted as he clung to a shoulder harness and gazed out the sliding door of the Seahawk. "There are men with bazookas or something like that over there...."

Mandera was pointing at a pair of terrorists armed with Soviet-made RPG-7 rocket launchers, positioned behind a battered old sedan. Ngong fired a rapid burst at the pair. Machine gun bullets hammered the body of the sedan. One terrorist ducked low, but the other tried to aim his rocket launcher at the Seahawk. Two 7.62 mm rounds smashed through his jawbone and punctured his throat and neck. The terrorist dropped his RPG-7 and fell from view.

Ngong tried to fire his L7A2 at the other terrorist with a rocket launcher, but before he could do so the pilot abruptly swung the chopper in a wide arc to the north. The sergeant triggered the machine gun and fired a dozen unaimed rounds at the ground below. Two terrorists with automatic rifles were positioned in the area. Four slugs chewed through the chest of one gunman while the other fired his AK-47 at the Seahawk.

Kalashnikov rounds pelted the chopper. Ngong gasped as a stray projectile sizzled past his ear and tugged at a strap of his shoulder harness. At least one round whined and ricocheted within the copter. Ngong clenched his teeth, closed his eyes and prayed for survival.

"I thought we were done for, Captain." Ngong sighed with relief after the sour song of bullets against metal ceased. "Guess it's not our time yet...."

He turned to Captain Mandera. The NSS officer hung limp in his shoulder rig. His head was bowed, and blood dripped from what remained of his face. The back of Mandera's skull had been punched open by an exit wound from which brains had spattered against the ceiling of the Seahawk.

"Oh, no," Ngong whispered in a broken voice.

A large projectile suddenly streaked past the Seahawk. A long white tail trailed the warhead like a miniature comet. It narrowly missed the rotor blades and sailed into a high arch, peaked and descended to earth. Fortunately for Ngong and the chopper pilot, the RPG-7 round was not a heat-seeking missile. It exploded when it struck the ground and, ironically, it killed the terrorist sniper who had shot Captain Mandera.

The terrorist with the rocket launcher laid down his weapon and gathered up the RPG-7 of his slain comrade. He braced the second launcher across his shoulder and started to raise it.

A trio of 9 mm bullets suddenly smashed into the fanatic's skull. His brains spilled across the roof of the sedan and his body fell sideways. As he died, a muscle twitch triggered his RPG-7. The rocket burst from the launcher muzzle and streaked across the compound, crashing into a terrorist billet. The building exploded in a violent shower of splinters and bloody remains of slain enemies.

Rafael Encizo had taken out the rocket-launching terrorist with his MP-5. The Cuban was the first member of Phoenix Force to reach the heart of the plantation, though the other three were not far behind. Encizo jogged to check out the slain terrorists by the sedan as his teammates covered his progress.

From the cover of another billet a group of terrorists fired at Encizo. Bullets tore up geysers of dirt near the Cuban's feet as he ran to the riddled car. He dived forward, hit the ground and shoulder-rolled to cover. His heart was racing, but his hands remained steady as he gathered up one of the RPG-7 rocket launchers. A crate of missiles for it was under one of the corpses.

Calvin James fired his grenade launcher and lobbed a 40 mm blaster into the billet a group of gunmen were using for cover. The explosion shattered the house and pitched the bodies of enemy troops into the open. Most were already dead, but three started to struggle to their feet.

By this time the Seahawk was again approaching the thick of the battle. Sergeant Ngong hosed the three survivors with machine-gun slugs. Their bloodied bodies would never rise again.

Two terrorists fired machine pistols at the Seahawk. Their shots were good. Bullet holes appeared in the Plexiglas windscreen, and the pilot twisted in the cockpit, his face contorted in agony. The chopper began a sharp descent, while the injured pilot struggled with the cyclic controls and pumped the rudder pedals. The main undercarriage wheels touched down hard, and the chopper skidded across the ground and headed for the main house.

Sergeant Ngong cut himself free of his harness and leaped from the helicopter just before it crashed into the building. The rotor blade sliced into a wall and the chopper swerved and smashed lengthwise against the adobe brick. Ngong limped toward Phoenix Force.

"Get down!" James shouted when he saw a gunman about to shoot the NSS sergeant in the back.

Ngong fell flat on his belly and covered his head with his arms. Half a dozen parabellum rounds from the terrorist's Sterling machine pistol burned the air above Ngong's prone form. The gunman cursed and tried to adjust his aim, but Calvin James already had the bastard in his sights. The hardass from Chicago triggered his M-16 and pumped a trio of 5.56 mm messengers into the terrorist's face.

An instant later a gunman appeared at the doorway of the main house and fired an Uzi at James. The Phoenix pro ducked behind the cover of an outbuilding. Nine mm slugs splintered wood from his shelter, but failed to reach the American. Gary Manning fired his FAL and placed three 7.62 mm rounds in the Uzi-gunner's chest. The guy dropped his weapon and toppled backward across the threshold.

"Everybody stay down!" Encizo warned as he aimed the RPG-7 at the twisted remains of the Seahawk crumpled against the side of the main house.

The Cuban fired the rocket launcher. The Soviet missile zoomed from the muzzle and collided with its target. The helicopter exploded, its fuel tanks erupting to contribute to the destruction that knocked down a wall of the house and sent half the roof caving in.

David McCarter had been crawling toward the main house. When the dust began to settle, he rose and dashed forward. The Briton hurled a flash-bang grenade through a window. The concussion blast shattered glass from two windows and sent a dazed African gunsel tumbling over a sill. McCarter hardly glanced at the wounded man as he mounted the porch and charged through the door.

Plaster dust drifted inside the building like gritty fog. The British ace waved the swirling haze from his face with his left hand as he clenched the pistol-grip of his MAC-10 in his right. The bodies of terrorists littered the floor. One man had been crushed by a fallen beam from the ceiling, and another lay dead with a splinter as thick as a man's finger buried in his throat. Stray bullets had killed a few others, and a bloody cluster of severed arms and decapitated torsos revealed that at least two opponents had been blown apart by the exploding copter.

McCarter did not falter at the gory sight, but merely stepped around the bloodied debris. He slid under the sagging beam to look in the room beyond, which appeared to have suffered a minimum of damage from the explosion. The Briton approached the doorway carefully. He peered around the corner, exposing only one eye and the muzzle of his Ingram machine pistol.

Chou Ziyang stood in the middle of the room, a Chinese Tokarev pistol in his fists. He aimed the weapon at McCarter, who ducked back and prepared to fire his MAC-10. The Briton held his fire when he heard only the rattle of stubborn metal parts.

McCarter guessed what had happened. In his opinion, the Tokarev was a piece of shit that would jam if you so much as looked at it too hard. Once more he peered around the edge of the door and saw Chou struggling with the slide of the Tokarev. An unfired cartridge jutted from the chamber and blocked the slide.

"Drop it," McCarter ordered. "It's no good anyway."

"Yes," Chou agreed grimly as he tossed the Tokarev aside. The Chinese raised his hand to shoulder level. "I suppose I should congratulate you."

"Lie down on your belly and place your hands at the small of your back," McCarter instructed, pointing the Ingram at his opponent. "No tricks. I spent some time in Hong Kong and I know how tricky some of you blokes can be. Don't bother trying any of your martial arts moves out on me."

"I'm not foolish enough to resist a man with a gun," Chou said as he passively adopted a front-leaning position on the floor.

McCarter did not trust the man. Chou was too passive, too calm. He would try something, McCarter was sure of that. If the Briton were in Chou's place, he would do the same thing.

A large picture of Mao Tse-tung in a silver frame on the wall caught McCarter's eye.

"Jesus," he hissed, noting the incense burner and the copy of *The Quotations of Chairman Mao Tse-tung* on a table beneath the portrait. "What are you? Red Guard?"

"You say that as if it was a disease," Chou remarked.

"That's not a bad description of the Red Guard," McCarter replied. "It's a goddamn pack of mad dogs, brainwashed by that bastard on the wall."

"Wang pu tan!" Chou snarled. "How dare you speak so of the greatest man who ever lived! Mao is the greatest Marxist-Leninist and social reformer the world has ever known."

"Is that what this was all about?" McCarter scoffed. "You killed all those innocent people and tried to start a conflict between the Soviets and the Western governments because you have some idiot scheme of starting a Maoist revolution in Kenya? You did this because of your fanatic hero worship of a dead dictator?"

"You do not understand," Chou stated. "You are an English bootlicker. How could you begin to understand?"

"I'm just lucky, I guess," McCarter replied with a shrug.

A footfall warned McCarter that someone lurked behind him. The Briton turned sharply and saw Li Yuann with a Sterling machine pistol in his fists. McCarter snap-aimed and triggered the Ingram at the same instant as the Sterling snarled. Three bullets hissed past McCarter's left ear, sending an arctic shiver up his spine. The Phoenix fighter nailed Li Yuann with five 9 mm rounds that split his face from chin to hairline. The back of Li's skull exploded, and the Chinese collapsed to the floor in a lifeless heap.

As McCarter spun to face his other Chinese opponent, Chou Ziyang leaped from the floor. His foot lashed out and kicked the Ingram from McCarter's grasp. Landing nimbly on the balls of his feet, Chou slashed the side of his hand into the Briton's chest. The blow hit McCarter under the breastbone and sent him staggering backward into a wall.

The Briton gasped air into his winded lungs as Chou launched a powerful sidekick for McCarter's abdomen. The hard side of McCarter's hand chopped Chou's ankle to block the kick, and the Briton adroitly hooked a toe kick to Chou's kidney.

The Chinese hissed with pain. Swiftly he whipped a backfist across McCarter's face. The Briton tasted blood and staggered from the blow. Chou stamped the heel of a palm into the side of McCarter's head and knocked him to the floor. The Asian raised his foot and prepared to stomp the Briton's head into pulp.

In a flash McCarter's legs lashed out in a scissors kick and trapped Chou's stationary leg. The Briton turned his hips and yanked Chou off balance. The Chinese fell on his back, but swiftly rolled backward and jumped to his feet. McCarter also rose and started to reach for his Browning Hi Power.

The pistol cleared leather but got no farther. Lunging forward, Chou seized the Briton's wrist with one hand and drove the stiffened fingers of his other hand under McCarter's ribs. A piercing pain lanced the Briton's side. Chou twisted the wrist hard and McCarter's pistol fell to the floor.

McCarter's left fist streaked in a fast jab to Chou's face. The Asian's head recoiled from the punch, and McCarter pulled his wrist free. The Briton quickly rammed an elbow to his opponent's sternum and slashed a karate chop at Chou's throat.

The Asian blocked the stroke with a forearm and slashed the side of his other hand at the nape of McCarter's neck. His head stinging with pain, the Briton groaned and fell to one knee. Chou raised his hand and prepared to strike the vulnerable seventh vertebrae to break McCarter's neck.

The Briton whipped a backfist between Chou's legs. The Chinese gasped in agony as bile rose into his throat. Chou swung both hands at McCarter's throat, fingers arched like claws. The Briton rose swiftly and slammed his forearms against the insides of Chou's wrists to block the attack.

McCarter's head snapped forward and butted Chou on the bridge of the nose. The Asian's knees buckled. McCarter seized Chou's jacket front and pumped a knee into his opponent's battered groin. Chou doubled up, nearly choking on the vomit lodged in his throat. Quickly McCarter wrapped his right arm around the Asian's neck to form a front headlock. He seized Chou's shoulder with one hand and Chou's wrist with the other to create a noose with his forearms.

Then McCarter sharply turned his shoulders. There was a dull snap, and Chou's body went limp. McCarter had broken the Asian's neck. He released his grasp and the former Red Guard slumped to the floor.

"Well," the Briton said, gasping to catch his breath. He gazed up at the picture of Mao and tried again to speak. "Well...I hope...you're satisfied."

19

The two young men in white uniforms mounted the narrow stairwell. Hospital visiting hours had ended at ten o'clock that evening. Lother Zeigler glanced at his wristwatch. Ten after one in the morning. They had waited long enough.

"Check the corridor," Zeigler whispered to Jurgen Tauber. "We must know how many opponents we'll have to deal with, including hospital staff and the federal agents protecting the Jew."

Tauber nodded, eased open the door and stepped into the corridor. Although half the overhead lights had been turned off, the hall was not dim. At the nurses' station, two nurses and a bleary-eyed young intern were talking softly about their problems with the hospital administration. The corridor beyond appeared to be deserted except for the two federal agents stationed in front of the door to Yakov Katzenelenbogen's room.

"How's it goin'?" Tauber inquired as he approached the nurses' desk.

"What are you doing here, Bob?" Mary Beth Meadows asked in surprise. The nurse knew Tauber by his assumed name of Robert Pelson. She glanced at the wall clock. "You went off duty hours ago."

"They called me in for graveyard," Tauber said with a shrug. "You wanna hear something stupid? Nobody seems to know what floor I'm supposed to be working on tonight. I thought you might know. Am I supposed to work here tonight?"

"What for?" The intern rolled his eyes. "There's nothing to do tonight, nothing's happening on this floor, fella. Just those two government jokers hanging around as if they expect a gang of terrorists to come charging down the corridor any minute. Wonder who that guy is they're guarding."

"Probably a high official from the IRS," Tauber joked. "They'd better protect him. I bet he's got a lot of enemies."

"Yeah," the intern agreed with a smile. "If anybody comes for the guy, maybe we should let them have him."

"I could call the head nurse," Meadows suggested. "Maybe she could tell you what you're supposed to do, Bob."

"That's okay," Tauber assured her. "I'm gonna get a cup of coffee and a smoke. Then I'll check with Baker in Emergency. If they need me at all tonight, it's probably down there."

"It's been a pretty quiet night so far," the intern stated. "Maybe we'll be lucky and it'll stay that way."

"One can but hope," Tauber replied. "See you later."

Tauber headed for the stairs and met with Zeigler. Quietly they discussed the situation. Lother Zeigler gathered up his black AWOL bag and unzipped it. The Nazis were prepared for emergencies. The case contained two Walther pistols with silencers, two Mark II hand grenades, a roll of thick electrical tape and a lead-filled sap. Zeigler quickly outlined a plan of action, and Tauber nodded in agreement.

Both men stepped through the stairwell door and entered the corridor. The intern and the two nurses were surprised to see Bob Pelson return so soon with another orderly. Zeigler and Tauber smiled as they strolled to the desk.

"Not only did Baker send me back," Tauber stated, "he sent the new guy with me, too."

"The name is Smith," Zeigler said with a nod, his hands behind his back. "I started working here two days ago."

"This is nuts," the intern complained as Tauber stepped behind him. "Call Baker and find out what the hell's going on."

"Forget Baker," Nurse Meadows replied as she reached for the phone. "Dr. Kyler is in the building. I'll have her sort this out . . ."

"Don't touch the phone," Zeigler hissed as he raised his hands to chest level. The Nazi's back was turned to the bodyguards stationed at Katz's door. They could not see what he held in his fists.

But Mary Beth Meadows, the intern and the nursing assistant saw the grenade in Zeigler's right fist. He pulled out the pin and held the explosive weapon tightly, pressing the spoon down. Tauber pushed the button on a NATO military knife. The four-inch blade snapped into place, and Tauber jabbed the steel point at the intern's right kidney.

"Don't be a hero," Tauber whispered. "This is no game. We'll kill you all and sacrifice our own lives if we have to. We really don't give a fuck. Understand?"

The intern nodded.

"If this is a joke..." Nurse Meadows began.

"It isn't, Mary Beth," the intern declared as he raised his arms. "Bob has a knife at my back."

"Put your hands flat on the desk," Zeigler ordered in a soft voice. "Move them and I'll blow you to pieces. Remain perfectly still and keep your mouths shut."

"What's this all about?" Nurse Meadows demanded, remaining very calm in the face of danger. The nursing assistant started to tremble and gasp in panicked breaths. "Get hold of yourself, Betty. I don't think they'll hurt us if we just do as they say."

"Listen to her, Betty," Tauber said. "You start screaming and we'll all die together."

"Okay now," Zeigler began, "very slowly move to the wall on your right. Face the corner so you'll be out of sight of the men down the hallway. No tricks. Just do it."

The nurses followed orders without debate. The intern began to move, but Tauber gripped his arm and pressed the knife blade harder at his kidney. The intern froze.

"You wait here," the Nazi ordered.

Zeigler pushed the pin back into the grenade and moved behind the desk. He shoved the weapon into a pocket and raised his shirt to remove a Walther PPK with silencer from his waistband. The Nazi held the weapon in his lap and nodded at Tauber.

Jurgen Tauber walked down the corridor toward the two feds at Katz's door. Special Agents Farley and Renko had noticed the activity at the nurses' station, but had not seen anything menacing about it. They had also seen Bob Pelson working on that floor before, so they were not concerned when he approached.

"There's a phone call for you fellas," Tauber told them. "Somebody named Brown."

"I'll take it," Farley announced.

Tauber continued down the corridor and entered a room two doors from Katz's quarters. The Nazi glanced at the sleeping patient in the bed. She was lucky. If she had been awake, Tauber would have killed her with his knife. The woman appeared to be sedated and sleeping soundly. Tauber nodded, satisfied with the way the plan was going so far. He raised his shirt and drew a silenced Walther pistol from the small of his back.

Agent Farley walked to the nurses' station. He noticed the intern standing rigidly in front of the desk and then saw the two nurses facing the wall. The agent suddenly realized he was walking into a trap and reached for the .38 revolver under his coat.

Lother Zeigler aimed the Walther with both hands and fired two rounds. The silenced pistol coughed, and a pair of 7.65 mm slugs crashed into Farley's forehead. The agent folded onto the floor.

When Agent Renko saw his partner fall he reached for his own weapon. But Jurgen Tauber had emerged from the room of the sleeping patient and had crept behind the unsuspecting agent. Now he fired the Walther into the back of Renko's skull. The agent fell to one knee as Tauber came nearer and pumped a second round through the man's head.

YAKOV KATZENELENBOGEN SAT at his desk inside the room. He had been reading a newsletter printed in braille and listening to a Mozart tape, but he heard a familiar *phut-phut* from the corridor. The sound was faint, muted by the door. Katz slid his fingers along the desk top to the tape recorder and pressed the stop button.

The Israeli sat quietly in the dark room, his eyes bandaged and encased in a darkness deeper than the shadows that surrounded him. His prosthesis was in the desk drawer, but he had no weapon in the conventional sense. As he eased the drawer open and reached for the artificial arm, Katz listened carefully.

In the corridor, Zeigler and Tauber had quickly bound and gagged the intern and the two nurses. None of them offered any resistance, but Zeigler slugged them with the lead-filled sap, anyway. He clubbed the nurses as hard as he hit the intern, across the base of the skull, not caring whether the blows were fatal or caused lasting brain damage.

The Nazis dragged the bodies of the slain federal agents to the nurses' station and hid the corpses behind the desk. Then they put their pistols away and headed for Katz's room. Neither man felt he needed a gun to deal with a middle-aged blind man with only one arm. Besides, Zeigler wanted Katz's death to include a personal touch that a bullet lacked.

Zeigler pushed open the door and flicked on the wall switch. The overhead light came on. Yakov Katzenelenbogen sat on the edge of the bed, his cane across his lap. The right sleeve of his pajama shirt was rolled up to his shoulder and he was tightening the straps of the prosthesis attached to the stump of his arm.

"Relax, Jew," Zeigler hissed. "You aren't going anywhere except to hell—where all you Christ-killing subhumans will eventually find yourselves."

"You talk like a Nazi," Katz commented as he stood, his hand resting on the crutch handle of his cane. "But I don't recognize your voice."

"Perhaps you recognize the name of General Adolf Zeigler," the young fanatic replied. "He was my father."

"There are two of you?" Katz heard Tauber's footsteps behind Zeigler. "You, Zeigler, must be a far greater coward than your father was. He wasn't a very brave man, but he wouldn't need help to shoot down an unarmed blind man."

"You filthy Jew bastard!" Zeigler growled. "We're not going to shoot you. Your death will not be that quick, nor that merciful. If you were not already blind, I would gouge out your eyes and squash them like grapes. So I'll have to settle for cutting you to pieces.''

Katz heard the metallic click of a steel blade snapping into locked position. The sound came from where he know the second man stood, not from Zeigler's position. Katz listened carefully to Tauber's footsteps as they moved toward the left. Another click told him that Zeigler, too, had pressed the button of a knife. He pictured the steel blades waving in the hands of his invisible opponents.

Guided by the sound made by the second knife blade snapping open, Katz suddenly slashed his cane at Zeigler in a sweeping stroke. Katz's sudden offensive took Zeigler and Tauber by surprise. They had not expected him to strike out with such remarkable accuracy without the benefit of eyesight.

The cane cracked against Zeigler's wrist and sent the knife hurtling from his numb fingers. Katz immediately turned and thrust his cane in the direction where he thought Tauber stood. The end of the walking stick scraped Tauber's hip. The Nazi cursed and lunged with his knife.

The cane had missed its mark, but nevertheless Katz had located his opponent with the wooden shaft. The Israeli raised his cane to ward off Tauber's attack and sent a kick to the Nazi's side. Tauber groaned and fell sideways. Katz leaped across the room and bounced against the wall near the door.

Assuming Katz was trying to escape, the Nazis charged after him. Katz slid his cane along the wall, found the light switch and snapped it off. Swiftly and silently he padded on bare feet toward his attackers, then dropped to one knee.

Katz lashed out with the cane in his left fist and extended his prosthetic arm like a lance. Hard wood clipped one opponent across the shins, and the metal "hand" of the prosthesis caught the other Nazi in the gut. The first man gasped with surprise and tumbled to the floor. The other groaned from the stiff punch to the belly and Katz hammered him with the handle of the cane. The blow struck something solid, probably a well-developed biceps, and the second opponent fell to his knees beside Katz. Quickly Katz swung a backhand stroke with the prosthesis and hit a solid round object. Katz grunted with the satisfaction of having smacked the bastard in the head.

"Lother?" the other man whispered as he approached Katz, unsure who was moving in the darkness in front of him.

Katz replied by slashing his cane at the man's voice. The hardwood struck Jurgen Tauber in the face. He groaned and struck out with his knife. Katz felt the man's forearm bump the cane, and he pushed the stick hard and swung a kick at Tauber's legs. The Nazi said *"scheiss"* as he tripped. Katz grabbed the center of his cane and chopped the handle across the fallen man's torso.

Tauber moaned, but managed to grab the cane with one hand and to slash upward with the knife. Sharp steel sliced Katz's pajama top and skin. The wound was shallow, but Katz felt blood trickle from his belly as he released the cane and retreated.

As he rose from the floor, Tauber swung the cane wildly. Katz backed away from the sound of the whirling stick, until his legs touched the bed. He threw himself across the mattress and rolled to the other side.

The Israeli stayed put as the two Nazis groped around in the dark. Tauber tagged Zeigler with the cane. The other Nazi reacted with a vicious karate side-kick that knocked Tauber across the room. Katz smiled as he listened to his opponents fighting with each other, but he realized they would soon locate him.

The sound of Tauber's body striking the wall gave Katz a target, and he grabbed his pillow from the bed and tossed it toward Tauber. The pillow brushed past the confused Nazi, who swung the cane wildly and thrust his knife desperately at the unseen opponent. He nearly clubbed Zeigler with the cane and did slash him with the knife blade.

Zeigler cursed when sharp steel cut his forearm. He whipped a backfist to Tauber's face and knocked his partner to the floor, then rushed to the door and found the light switch. Katz heard the click of the switch and realized the lights were on again.

Katz quickly scooped up the mattress from his bed and used it as a shield as he charged over the springs and headed toward the Nazis. Tauber raised the cane and stabbed the knife into the mattress, which protected Katz from wood and sharp steel. The Israeli kept moving and ducked low to ram the Nazi at the legs.

Tauber fell to the floor, but Zeigler seized the end of the mattress and yanked if from Katz's grip. Zeigler stepped forward and slammed a fist to the Israeli's face. The punch sent Katz hurtling backward into the desk. His hand brushed the backrest of the chair.

As he heard Zeigler close in, Katz yanked the chair from under the desk and shoved it forward. It tipped over onto the floor and clipped Zeigler's shins. The Nazi yelped with surprise as he tripped and fell against the desk. Katz grabbed the man's shirt and clubbed him between the shoulder blades with the prosthesis.

By then Tauber was up off the floor and attacking. He had abandoned the cane and now lunged with the knife. Katz sensed the attack coming and raised his prosthesis, but Tauber's knife stroke slid under it. The sharp blade cut Katz along the rib cage.

Katz clenched his teeth in pain and grabbed for the arm above the offending knife. He twisted Tauber's wrist to direct the knife blade away and jammed the end of his prosthesis under the Nazi's jaw.

The Israeli was accustomed to a prosthesis with powerful steel hooks and springs that were capable of tearing a man's throat open or crushing bone. The artificial arm supplied by the hospital was not designed for combat. Katz dug the hooks of his prosthesis into the hollow of Tauber's throat. He tangled his legs around the Nazi's nearest leg, forcing Tauber off balance. Both men hit the floor, Katz on top with the prosthesis still lodged in his opponent's throat.

The hooks of the device sank deeper as the Nazi's throat caved in. Katz felt Tauber's body convulse, and warm liquid spewed from the Nazi's mouth. Blood splashed Katz's artificial arm. Jurgen Tauber sprawled dead on the floor.

As Katz started to rise, a hard kick to the ribs knocked him down. Lother Zeigler dropped on top of the Israeli and pinned the prosthesis under his knee. He seized Katz's left arm and locked the wrist under his arm, gripping the Israeli's elbow to hold the arm stationary.

"Schweinhund!" Zeigler snarled as he hammered his fist into Katz's face. "I'm going to crush you like a maggot!"

Katz's head throbbed painfully. The black void of his blindness was interrupted by spots of brilliant white and orange lights. Lother Zeigler had a punch most middleweight contenders would have envied. Katz felt dizzy, but his survival instincts, honed by years of training and experience, continued to function.

He bent a knee and slammed it into the small of Zeigler's back. His larger, younger and physically stronger opponent simply grunted and crashed his knuckles into the center of Katz's face, breaking his nose. Blood filled the Israeli's sinuses, and his skull felt as if it might split open. From the end of a long tunnel, he heard the familiar voice of a woman utter a soft cry.

"Oh, my God!" Julia Kyler exclaimed when she entered Katz's room.

One man lay dead. Another had Katz pinned to the floor and seemed determined to beat her patient to death. Julia rushed forward and seized Zeigler from behind. She realized the man was homicidal and she recalled her knowledge of basic anatomy and the restraint tactics learned when she'd worked in psycho wards in the past.

Julia grabbed the Nazi's neck and squeezed, fingers pressed to the carotid arteries and thumbs jammed in the mastoid. If she could cut off the blood supply to his brain for about thirty seconds, he would pass out.

Surprised by Julia's attack, Zeigler felt disoriented, but he was too big and strong not to put up a fight. He jabbed an elbow at her, but missed as she braced herself between his shoulder blades. The Nazi reached back and grabbed her hair, but Julia held onto his neck. Zeigler finally had to release Katz's arm to use his other hand to pry the woman's fingers from his carotid.

Julia cried out as Zeigler yanked her hair forcibly and pulled her right hand from his neck. He hauled her about and shoved hard. Julia fell into the bed and slid to the floor. Zeigler glared at her, his expression telling her that he would deal with her as soon as he finished with Katz.

Then a hand appeared in front of Zeigler's face. Katz clawed the fingers of his left hand over the Nazi's face. They found the twin curves of soft tissue on each side of Zeigler's nose. Katz stabbed in the fingers as hard as he could.

Lother Zeigler screamed as a finger crowded an eyeball out of its socket. The orb dangled, suspended by the optic nerve. Blood welled within the socket and oozed down his cheek like crimson tears. Zeigler was immediately plunged into a terrible world of monstrous pain and pitch-black blindness.

The Nazi howled in agony and clasped his hands to his face. A palm touched the wet-olive shape and texture of his eyeball. Horror accompanied pain and Zeigler shrieked again. He did not even feel Katz's hand strike. The "panther punch" stroke drove the bent knuckles into Zeigler's throat. The thyroid cartilage collapsed and the windpipe caved in. Zeigler flopped on his back, convulsed briefly and slid into shock. A few seconds later, the fanatical son of General Adolf Zeigler was dead.

"Yakov!" Julia cried as she knelt beside the battered Phoenix Force commander. "Don't move yet. You might have internal injuries."

"Did I get the bastards?" Katz asked thickly through a split lip.

"You got them," she assured him.

"Are they both dead?" the Israeli demanded.

"Yes, damn it," Julia replied in an unsteady voice.

"Okay," Katz said with a sigh. "Now I'll relax."

20

"We leave you alone for a few days and look what happens," David McCarter commented as he sat beside Katzenelenbogen's bed.

"You should see the other guys," Katz replied with a weak grin. His lip was still swollen and a lump appeared at the bridge of his nose beneath the bandages that still covered his eyes. "I hear your mission went pretty well without me."

"We managed," Gary Manning said dryly. "But we sure could have used you, Yakov."

"Hal tells us you were the one who suggested the computer check on possible extremist groups operating in Kenya," Rafael Encizo commented. "That led us to suspect the two Chinese who turned out to be the masterminds behind the plot. So you were still a team player on this mission, Yakov. Even from here."

"You fellas would have figured it out eventually," Katz assured them. "I knew you could handle things without me."

"We work best as a five-man team with you in command," Calvin James told him. "The bandages come off today?"

"That's right," Katz confirmed. "Then we'll know one way or the other."

"You seem pretty confident you'll regain your vision," Manning commented. "You're certainly in better spirits than you were just before we left for Kenya."

"Killing ODESSA agents must be good medicine for you," McCarter stated. "But taking on two opponents while blindfolded—isn't that showing off?"

"I wouldn't care to do it again," Katz said, smiling. "But to answer Gary's remark, I'm not at all confident I'll be able to see. That's still fifty-fifty, which is fair odds."

"Better than we're used to taking on," Encizo commented.

"Right," Katz said with a nod. "If all goes well, we'll handle the next mission together. If not, I don't want you guys to worry about me. I'll be okay. I can already read braille and get around fairly well in the dark. I'm not going to curl up and die if I'm still blind."

"What'll you do, Yakov?" James asked.

"Teach intelligence courses for some espionage outfit," Katz answered. "Write books, learn to operate computers, work as a translator for a government agency. The important thing is, I'll still be living and growing in every way possible. That's the best we can do on this planet. Keep living and not give up. Learn as much as possible and always keep trying to learn more. *Live* as much as possible and keep trying to *live* more."

The door opened. Julia Kyler entered and removed a pair of scissors from her pocket. She made certain the venetian blinds were closed.

"Hello, Yakov," she said, and then looked toward the other men gathered in the room. "Are you ready to have your bandages removed?"

"I'm eager to find out the verdict," Katz answered. "And these men can stay. They're friends of mine."

"I know. They introduced themselves to me a while ago," Julia answered. "If they're here, they may as well make themselves useful. I want one man by the window. When I cut away the first layers of the bandage, open the blinds slowly. We don't want to risk damaging Yakov's eyes by exposing them to bright light immediately."

"I understand," Manning assured her as he walked to the window.

"And I need a man by the wall switch," Julia continued, "to switch off the lights after I cut the first bandage."

"Better let me handle that," James remarked. "I've had medical training. It is a hospital light switch, you know."

"What do we do?" Encizo asked, referring to himself and David McCarter.

"Just sit down and be quiet," Julia replied as she squeezed Katz's hand. "Ready, Yakov?"

"Go ahead," he assured her.

The doctor inserted the scissors and cut the first layer of bandage. She began to unwrap it and called for James to switch off the light. The black warrior followed instructions. Julia continued to unwind the bandage.

"Open the blinds just a crack," she told Manning. "We want very dim light for now."

The Canadian eased the cord of the venetian blinds and a faint ribbon of light appeared. Julia kept removing the bandages. At last, only two cotton balls covered Katz's eyes.

"Okay," she announced. "This is it."

Julia removed the cotton. "Open your eyes," she told Yakov Katzenelenbogen.

His lids parted slowly. The room was dark and blurred to Katz's vision, yet a slight glow of light hovered among the black haze. He blinked twice. The room came into focus. The light was clearly visible. The shapes of heads and shoulders were outlined in the dimness.

"I can see," Katz announced with relief. "I can see."

"Let in a little more light, please," Julia instructed.

Manning eased the slats of the blinds farther open. The increased light flowed into the room, and Katz clearly saw the faces of his fellow Phoenix Force commandos.

Manning was still stationed by the window, features frozen in a poker face to conceal his emotions. James leaned against the door, a wide grin plastered on his dark features. McCarter stood and held up three fingers. He pointed at them, waiting for Katz to tell him how many he saw. Katz held up three fingers in response. Encizo sighed with relief and smiled, glad the ordeal was finally over.

Katz turned to Julia. He saw her face for the first time. She smiled weakly and her intelligent brown eyes gazed back at him through round lenses.

"I was right," he said gently. "You are beautiful."

"Maybe we'll have to check your eyes some more," she replied.

"Don't be silly," Katz told her.

"When can he leave, Doctor?" James inquired.

"He can sign out today," Julia replied. "You need to get back to your life, Yakov."

"I owe you a great deal," Katz began.

"I think we're even," she assured him, looking down at the floor. "Well, we'll need this room for other patients...."

"You'll see me again," Katz promised, taking her hand in his.

"Uh...we'll meet you in the hall," Encizo declared as he headed for the door, aware that Katz and Julia needed some privacy.

"What?" McCarter complained. "We're right here—"

"Let's go," Manning urged, jerking his head toward the door.

"Oh?" Then McCarter smiled. "Right. Let's all meet in the corridor."

"Mr. Brown says he'll need to see us tomorrow for a complete report," James added. "I think something else has come up, too."

"Tell Brown I'll be there," Katz assured him.

The other four men left the room. Julia sat on the edge of the bed, and Katz leaned forward and kissed her lightly on the lips.

"You're going back to whatever you do." She sighed. "And you can't tell me anything about it except it can be dangerous and you might get killed at any time. Right?"

"For now at least," Katz answered, "I'm afraid that's the way things are."

"You know you're insane," Julia complained.

"Probably," he said, smiling.

"And I'd have to be insane to have anything to do with you after what happened here last night," she added.

"Maybe," he said.

"Oh, hell." Julia sighed again. "You want to take me out for dinner tonight?"

"You pick the restaurant," Katz offered.

"We'll go to my place," Julia suggested. "Then we'll see if you can stand my cooking."

"You're on," he replied.

Available NOW!

DON PENDLETON's
MACK BOLAN

TROPIC HEAT

The probing tentacles of the drug network have crept far
enough into the streets of America. The only solution is
to cut the cancer out at the source. The only man equal
to the task is Mack Bolan!

SB-9R

**For the millions who can't read
Give the Gift of Literacy**

One out of five adults in North America
cannot read or write well enough
to fill out a job application
or understand the directions on a bottle of medicine.

**You can change all this by joining the fight
against illiteracy.**

For more information write to:
Contact, Box 81826, Lincoln, Neb. 68501
In the United States, call toll free: 800-228-3225

**The only degree you need
is a degree of caring**

TAKE 'EM NOW

FOLDING SUNGLASSES
FROM GOLD EAGLE

Mean up your act with these tough, street-smart shades. Practical, too, because they fold 3 times into a handy, zip-up polyurethane pouch that fits neatly into your pocket. Rugged metal frame. Scratch-resistant acrylic lenses. Best of all, they can be yours for only $6.99.

MAIL YOUR ORDER TODAY.

Send your name, address, and zip code, along with a check or money order for just $6.99 + .75¢ for postage and handling (for a total of $7.74) payable to Gold Eagle Reader Service. (New York and Iowa residents please add applicable sales tax.)

Remove from pouch...

unfold once...

unfold twice...

and they're ready to wear.

GOLD EAGLE

Gold Eagle Reader Service
901 Fuhrmann Blvd.
P.O. Box 1396
Buffalo, N.Y. 14240-1396

GES-1A

Offer not available in Canada.